Dead Again

Robert Gatto

Published by Trellis Publishing, 2021.

This is a work of fiction. Similarities to real people, places, or events are entirely coincidental.

DEAD AGAIN

First edition. July 12, 2021.

Copyright © 2021 Robert Gatto.

ISBN: 979-8224001354

Written by Robert Gatto.

DEAD AGAIN

ROBERT GATTO

Chapter One

"Sir, I need to speak with you urgently."

Doctor Zachary Jones straightened up from his microscope, rubbing his eyes and the back of his neck. He'd been working for the past fourteen hours without a break, with only a steady supply of coffee to keep him going. He was torn between being irritated at the interruption and relieved at the excuse to stop for a moment. His lab was silent, only the occasional distant scream could be heard echoing through the facility.

"What's up Mike?"

"The coroner from Zone 3 just couriered over a toxicology report from a recent murder victim, I think you should take a look at it."

Zach looked surprised at the statement. "He couldn't use email?"

Mike shook his head. "Signal's down again and the power's unstable. You're running on the backup generators but the rest of us are struggling with an intermittent supply again. God knows what the status is over in Zone 3. They're probably out altogether."

"I don't know if God has much to do with it anymore," Zach replied wryly. "I think we're on our own now."

Mike shrugged. "We're doing our best to rebuild things, but there just isn't enough people left to maintain everything, and not enough experts left for troubleshooting. We're still broadcasting the announcements over the air waves asking people to come, telling them we're offering employment, food and a place to stay, but nobody new has shown up for months. Contact with the scouting parties is obviously sketchy at best, but last we heard, they'd covered another seven states and hadn't found another living soul. It's looking like we gathered everyone up first time around."

"Dammit, we can't be the only people left in the whole of the United States! There's barely a thousand of us in each zone, that's less than six thousand people. With my contact with other bunkers before we lost them, I would estimate that the survivors at the time were in the region of thirty thousand at most. Last year, the population was three hundred and twenty *million*, and that was the ones that were registered and accounted for."

Mike sat down. "I know, it's crazy, the whole thing was a total shit storm, but right now, I need you look at this report."

"What's so special that a coroner can't handle his own murder case," Zach muttered, holding his hand out for the document. "It's not as if there's a lot of suspects left to choose from."

"I'd go straight to the toxicology report and look at the blood analysis if I were you," Mike advised.

Zach flipped the pages and finding the appropriate section, settled down to read. Ten minutes of silence ensued before Zach looked up with a panicked expression on his face.

"It can't be," he said helplessly.

"I was hoping I was wrong,"

It was the only answer Mike could give under the circumstances.

"Believe me, I'd have been happier to be interrupted for nothing, I can't believe this. I thought we'd wiped them out, apart from the ones we've got under lock and key."

To emphasize his point, another inhuman scream echoed through the underground facility where the public health department headquarters was now situated.

"You're absolutely certain that this is the same strain?"

"No doubt, but just in case we're acting like a couple of hysterical teenage girls, let's compare the print outs and double check."

After five minutes of silence while the two compared the reports, Zach stood. "We have to admit it, he was bitten or scratched by a zombie, he's infected with exactly the same strain of the virus that caused the first outbreak."

"That means there's still one out there, and we've led everyone to believe the streets are safe now."

"Not necessarily," Zach replied. "Is there any chance he's connected with research, that he would have been handling one of the captives for some reason? Maybe he just got careless."

"Afraid not, he was scanned completely clean before being dispatched to Zone 3, he's been working at the power plant ever since, trying to keep the grid up and running. That's where he was last seen."

"I hope everyone who handled the body stuck to procedure, else we've got another outbreak on our hands. Do you know if it's been incinerated yet?"

"The report doesn't say."

"Well for God's sake, find out, and make sure everyone who came into contact with this guy is thoroughly scanned. It's bad enough that there's still at least one running about out there, the last thing we need is the virus to be already on the inside."

"What are you going to do Zach?"

Zach sighed deeply. "First, I'm going to read this full report so I'm up on all the facts, after that, I've no idea."

Chapter Two

Zach maneuvered the motorbike through the city streets, carefully navigating what would have been a normal and noisy traffic jam but was now eerily silent and still. He'd decided that if he wanted a job done properly, he might as well do it himself. He was heading for Zone 3, but progress was slow. The cleanup operation that had been in place for months now were doing a good job of returning the city to a habitable state, but after the last of the zombies had been hunted down, all the remaining people found and scanned for the virus, they had been concentrating on removing bodies and incinerating them. Once that gruesome task was over, they'd begun on rubbish and rotting food, a huge problem since everyone's lives had been so suddenly and dramatically interrupted by the apocalypse that had hit them.

Half-eaten meals were left on tables, crawling with maggots and flies, fridges and freezers with no power were now filled with oozing mush which bore no resemblance to the groceries they'd once been, garbage cans and dumpsters crawled with rats and other vermin, omitting toxic stenches that polluted the very air around them. Zach shuddered to think of the stores and hypermarkets that had been filled with fresh produce. Yep, the cleanup crews had their work cut out for them, and they were making some pretty impressive headway, but they had more immediate worries than the graveyard of abandoned cars, trucks, vans and other vehicles that littered the roads, the result of the panic which had caused everyone to try and flee the city, hoping the virus was contained to one area and they could escape their fate.

Zach had initially hoped the same thing, but as a member of a government funded research team, he had been one of the first to hear that it was happening in every state countrywide, and spreading at a rate that no amount of forces could contain. The resulting loss of human life had been a greater tragedy than he could ever hope to express with mere words. He had gathered as much Intel as he could before lines of communication went down and it was every man for himself, isolated in their own small area. He and his team were aware of something most Americans were not, that every major city held at least one secure underground facility designed to protect the President in the event of terrorist attacks or natural disasters, wherever he may be at the time of their occurrence. Zach and his team had made their way there, with as much equipment as they could safely carry, moving rapidly under the cover of darkness and gathering up as many survivors as they could along the way. They sent out daily hunting parties, both to kill the zombies and to rescue as many of the human race as they could find uninfected. The bunker was designed to withstand anything anyone could possible imagine, and was stocked for the survival of hundreds for many years. Zach had immediately set up a broadcast over the airwaves giving detailed directions to safety. He also had the hunting parties place signs all over the city, begging people to come.

At first, people had arrived steadily. The bunker was spacious and equipped to outlast even nuclear radiation, but it had never been designed for so many. They had food and water, a state of the art medical facility and research lab, an extensive library, but what they lacked most severely was space. Living conditions became cramped and uncomfortable, so they had made plans to wipe out the threat and reclaim their society. They'd been through hardship and trauma, but through it, they had grown stronger. Some were already natural warriors, eager to unite and fight a common enemy, while others had to learn to ignore the horror and devastation they faced, overcoming their fears for the survival of the race. Zach was proud of each and every one. Slowly but surely, they had wiped out the zombies, taken the lives of those infected but not yet turned, and taken control of the city, gradually trying to return it to its former glory and reinstate all the systems that had been in place before the collapse of everything. Before communications went down, Zach had made contact with nine other bunkers across the country. They were occupied mostly by high level military personnel who had access codes, as many of their own teams that had survived, and rag tag bunches of survivors, just like Zach's own bunker. They had between them, coordinated a sweep of the USA with military precision, and had been in the midst of it when they lost contact. Only when Zach had completed his own instructions had he felt it safe for the people to return to life above ground, splitting the city into six manageable zones and allowing the people to choose their employment and place of residence.

Zach had worked tirelessly ever since, studying the virus, even requesting live samples of the creatures which were held in secure cages in the underground facility, in order to study them and to draw samples of blood and tissue to work with. He still had no idea where the virus had originated from, but his main purpose was to try and find a cure. Watching a loved one scream and beg for his life after being scanned positive for the virus, and having to ignore their pleas and end it for them before they could turn and infect others, was possibly the hardest thing to deal with throughout this horror. He was determined to put a stop to that, to find a cure that could halt the virus in its tracks and preserve the precious lives of the remaining few. His ultimate goal was one that could reverse it even after the infected had completely turned, but he'd settle for the first for now. Suddenly, he came across the sign that announced he was about to enter Zone 3, and he was surprised to find that he'd been lost in thought the whole journey. Concentrating now on the road, he headed for the crematorium which had been commandeered by the coroner to act as his new morgue, allowing for easy disposal of infected bodies. Nothing could be allowed to hang about for long these days.

Two guards stopped him at the door and he was required to remove his helmet and present some identification, only then was he allowed to pass. The coroner and the newly appointed chief of police were deep in conversation when he entered the room. Neither of them seemed surprised to see him. Zach didn't bother wasting time with pleasantries.

"Has the body been disposed of?"

"Of course," the coroner replied, shocked that he would be considered so incompetent as to not follow basic protocol.

"Good. Now gather up everyone, and I mean absolutely everyone, who had any contact with it at all, however minor."

"They've all been tested Zach," Pete, the chief of police told him gently.

"Yeah well, the virus can take a while to incubate and show itself. I'm testing them again."

"As you wish," Pete sighed, leaving to give the order.

"Might as well start with you Jimmy," Zach said, as he removed a pack of needles and a bulky handheld machine from his inside pocket. Reaching into the other side of his leather biker jacket, he removed a pack of gloves, a mask, a pair of goggles, and a batch of medical slides. He laid his equipment out on the desk and advanced on the coroner. Jimmy looked fearful as he rolled up his sleeve and presented his arm as Zach donned the safety equipment. He'd seen the gun strapped to Zach's hip as he'd pulled his jacket open, and he knew Zach wouldn't hesitate.

"I followed all the procedures," he whined as Zach drew a small amount of blood from his vein.

"Then you'll have nothing to worry about, will you?"

Zach proceeded to place a small drop of the blood on the slide, covered it with a sliver of membrane, and slid it into the machine. He pressed a few buttons then headed over to the bright yellow and black box marked for incineration and dropped the needle in. He returned and perched one hip on the edge of the desk, waiting for the machine to start throwing numbers at him. He had studied the virus extensively, he knew exactly the elevations and drops to look for to indicate that it was beginning to take hold, to slowly incubate, hiding in plain sight within its victim.

Jimmy was visibly sweating by the time Zach turned to him. "You're clean."

Jimmy sighed deeply with relief and swiped at his brow. "I'm the one who had most contact, I think testing the others is a waste of time and resources."

"Yeah, but the others might not have followed protocol as strictly as you. Look, Jim, we've got the same situation as we always had, people now concentrated again in the cities. You know how fast this happens, one infected person could wipe out all of Zone 3 in a matter of days or even hours, and you can bet your ass they'd move across the city searching for more food. The last thing you need is someone on the inside turning."

"I know, I know, it's better to be safe than sorry. It's just that they're all good men, I know each of them personally and I guess ... well, surviving this has created a bond ..."

Zach's expression softened. "I understand, I feel the same way, but until I can find a cure ..."

He left the rest of the words unspoken as the others began to enter the room. All of them were visibly relieved as they all tested clear of the virus that turned good men into drooling, slavering, mindless creatures that hungered for human flesh. They shuffled out of the room, no exuberance in their reprieve, only a thankfulness that left them almost weak with gratitude. Only Pete and Jimmy remained with Zach.

"Okay, so now that's over with, let's review this. The report said that the actual cause of death was a gunshot wound?"

"Yes, not an immediate kill shot, but he would have bled out within minutes," Pete replied.

"And nobody's coming forward to admit to the shooting?"

"We've questioned everybody and nobody seems to have any knowledge of it, and I believe 'em. The vic, Tom Smith, was last seen leaving the power plant at the end of his shift with his payment in food as usual. Reports all say he was same as ever, no weird moods, no unusual plans. He was found next morning by the Area West cleanup crew, who reported immediately. Location was on his way home but there was no sign of his food bag."

"So what's your theory?"

"Guess we got ourselves a lone drifter, who probably shot him for the food. We've been hunting but haven't managed to find him so he's probably moved on. I'm sending out an alert this morning to all areas to be on their guard and advise people not to carry food in plain sight."

"What about the bites?"

"There were only two, which is unusual, so my guess is that the creature was right there, getting in quick before Tom actually died. We know they don't eat dead flesh so I reckon it got the two bites in before he passed, then left him alone after that. I was hoping you could tell us why he didn't turn."

"Probably because he was so close to death and bleeding out," Zach shrugged. "The virus didn't have time to take hold and there wasn't enough blood still moving through the system to carry it."

"That makes sense," Jimmy interjected. "I had the same thoughts myself. I'm sorry he's dead but I'm glad he didn't turn into one of them."

"And you've found no sign of the creature either?"

"Nope, not a trace," Pete confirmed.

"Do you think it's possible the drifter and the zombie are one in the same? That maybe he was carrying the virus and turned just after the shooting?" Jimmy asked.

Zach considered the possibility. "It'd be one heck of a coincidence, but we know the virus takes about 48 hours to incubate fully and change the entire body, but when it does, it's almost instant. I guess it might be possible, he'd have been feeling pretty sick by then, maybe making him desperate enough to kill for food, putting his illness down to malnutrition or even starvation. But I'm not the only research facility with live samples, any reports of anybody losing one?"

"I sent people out to ask the very same question," Pete said. "So far, the ones that have come back have given a negative."

The three men digested the information in silence before Jimmy summed it up. "So either we've got a newly turned creature, or we've got one hell of a smart-assed zombie who's hiding out until opportunities arise."

"Either way, it's gotta be stopped or we'll have a second outbreak on our hands, and if it's one of our own guys, it'll retain some base memories of which areas of the city are active, and maybe even where the underground shelter is."

"Dear God, what are you gonna do, Zach."

"I'm gonna do what has to be done. Go out there and hunt the bastard down."

Chapter Three

Dressed as he was in head to toe black, biker leathers, from his heavy, buckled boots to his tight gloves, Zach looked more like a character from an action movie than the research scientist he was. The image was helped along with two guns at his side, held there by the holsters crossed over low on his hips. Another was concealed beneath his biker jacket in a shoulder holster and a long-range rifle was slung over his shoulder. In addition, his pockets bulged with ammo, and several knives were secured about his person.

"Are you still sure you want to do this alone? It wouldn't take more than a few hours to gather up and kit out a hunting party from all Zones. The military boys would handle this much better."

"We might not have hours, it's knocking off time soon and people are going to be on the streets heading home. This needs to be done now."

"At least let me come with you, it should be my job."

"Listen Pete, I know you mean well and I know you think you're better equipped for the job, and you're probably right, but if we're right in thinking this thing is deliberately hiding out and waiting for opportunities, then it's showing more intelligence than any of the others. Being alone might just offer it the opportunity it needs."

"So you're setting yourself up as bait?"

"If it comes to that, then yes, but hopefully I'll be bait that bites back."

"Just make sure you bite first."

Zach looked at Pete with a serious expression. "If I fail, I can rely on you to do the right thing?"

Pete returned his steady gaze. "I'd advise you keep the helmet on at all times, but if you get bitten or scratched, just make sure you take it off before you turn so we have a clear and clean head shot."

"Understood."

The men shook as they parted, each wondering if they would ever see the other again. Once out on the street, Zach checked his watch. The power plant was the largest place of employment in Zone 3 and there would be a shift change soon, he intended to be there, watching and following people home. They'd all been advised to travel in groups and carry weapons at all times, but there were always some that wouldn't heed the advice. If the thing was going to show itself, he wanted to be there to meet it.

He slid his leg over the bike, negotiating the panniers that had been added. One was filled with extra ammo for all his weapons, the other contained fresh water, a few energy bars and a walkie talkie in case he needed assistance out on the road. He could have done without the food, he could survive longer without it than the zombie would take to find another victim. If he began to starve before he had killed it, it would be all over for them anyway. The bike gave a powerful roar as he shot off into the growing dusk to head to the power plant.

Zach sat and watched from the shadows as people began to spill from the plant, talking and joshing each other as people who closely work together every day tend to do. It gave Zach a pang of sadness, it felt like a distant memory from a past life, something safe, something normal. At first, the people stuck to various groups as instructed, not quite as alert to their surroundings as Zach would have hoped, but at least heeding some of the warning. Zach followed on foot, and as the groups split to head in different directions, he tried to decide which one to stick with. He assessed them quickly. One group contained a guy that was on the outskirts, hanging back and not joining in the general conversation. Making his decision, Zach jogged back for the bike.

He'd quickly made it back and sure enough, the guy had split, walking off on his own down another street. Zach had figured him for a loner and as such, he'd probably picked a building to live in that didn't have any other occupants. He couldn't blame the guy, they'd all thought they were safe. Zach parked up the bike again and followed on foot, keeping to the shadows. He was relieved and disappointed when the guy made it safely to a large apartment building with no incident. The outer door was locked, and Zach caught a glimpse of the heavy steel reinforcement on the inside as the man unlocked it then swung it open and darted inside. He heard several locks and deadbolts click into place behind the man.

The loner was home safe, but Zach couldn't give up on the nagging feeling that he wouldn't be the only one to think he was the best chance for a zombie dinner. He decided to take a wander around the neighbourhood and see what he could throw up. With no real clue as to where to start, it seemed as good as any other. With the streets completely devoid of human life, Zach found himself with nothing to do but think as he walked and watched.

He had figured out a lot about the virus, but still didn't really understand it. The body seemed to be dead, the heart no longer beat, the organs didn't function, the flesh itself was dead, feeling no hot or cold, no pain, no injury too great to ignore completely. Yet they weren't dead in the sense we normally understood. To create that desire, that need for flesh, that never ending, driving hunger, synapses in the brain had to be firing. It was this that brought around the rudimentary intelligence, the memory patterns and the social interaction. He had watched them closely in captivity. They recognized their own new, strange species, accepted one another and even formed close bonds with some around them. They were protective of each other, and when given food, it might look like a horrendous, violent frenzy but if you looked closer, there was order to it and it was ensured that everyone got a partial share of what was available. As he'd watched, Zach had determined that more and more of the brain had seemed to fire up again over time, the sparks of certain areas kick starting others. Their intelligence increased the longer they survived. His main question now was whether the body would rot and fail before they regained full intelligence. If it didn't, even the ones in captivity posed a serious risk and would have to be destroyed, cutting Zach off from his research material.

He wasn't sure what he was dealing with here, but it seemed unlikely to be an older zombie, it had attacked the dying man too quickly. That seemed to imply one fairly recently formed, which meant to go undetected as it had, it had retained much more of the thinking process. Zach was pulled from his inner musings by a rustling noise from behind a set of dumpsters up ahead. He walked forward with more caution. If it was from inside, it was most likely rats. The vermin had survived and thrived on the rot and decay left behind by the people ripped from their daily lives. As he approached, he determined that the noise was coming from behind the bins, not inside.

He pulled one of the guns from the holster, releasing the safety and chambering a bullet, readying the gun to fire. He crept forward as quietly as he could in his heavy boots and flipped his visor down, protecting his eyes from possible infected blood spray or grasping, gouging fingers. He ducked down as he reached the bins, using them as cover as he slid along the front and round the side. He paused there, steadying his breathing and preparing himself for what he might find. With one final exhale, he turned the corner, gun raised, finger poised on the trigger.

A stray dog looked up at him and snarled, head low, a deep, menacing growl forming in its throat. It advanced one step, protecting whatever disgusting meal it had found. Zach almost laughed with relief but didn't want to be forced to shoot the dog if he caused it to attack. Other than the vermin and bugs that bred at rapid rates, animals were a scarce commodity in this new world. One day, this half-starved mutt might once again be someone's companion, their comfort in a lonely existence. He stepped away, allowing the animal to grab its prize and scarper.

He had surmised from his research and information that the virus didn't seem to effect any other species of life, although test subjects had been hard to come by. There were no reports or any zombie animals among the cities and those few he had captured to inject directly with infected blood had shown no ill effects and after a few months of observation, he had been able to release them with no concerns about the safety of the survivors. Similar reports from more rural areas with a wider range of species had confirmed their suspicions that it was only humans that turned. However, animals did seem to suffice as a meal for the zombies when they couldn't get to human flesh, but Zach had yet to fully understand their need to eat, since it didn't seem to sustain them in any way. It was just another piece of the puzzle, and hopefully, he would stay alive to solve it. His relieved reaction to the first tense moment had reminded him just how ill-equipped he was for his current task, his only advantage his basic understanding of the creatures he had been studying.

Chapter Four

Throughout the night, Zach searched, covering what he could working in an ever increasing circle out from the power plant, still certain that the concentration of people and the constant presence of human flesh was what had drawn the creature into Zone 3. He used the bike to cruise the streets, then would return to likely looking buildings to hunt through them. Despite his importance as a research scientist, he had not excluded himself from the original hunting parties so was not without some acquired skills, but every time he entered a building, he felt like a young boy poking a hornet's nest, aware of the danger he was stirring up but too intent on his purpose to stop.

As dawn rose, the only thing of interest he'd found was a recent camp, the empty food tins scattered around letting him know it belonged to a human, possibly the drifter that had shot Tom Smith. That was one for the police chief, he would report it later, if and when more pressing matters were resolved. Feeling the need to relieve himself after his long night, he headed to one of the many abandoned service stations. He wasn't sure which buildings had a water supply in Zone 3, so best to use a public urinal rather than a bathroom in a private residence and be unable to flush, the city had enough problems.

He entered cautiously, stepping over the fallen shelves and scattered goods that remained, mostly motor oils and cleaning products for cars that no longer ran or couldn't be negotiated through the blocked up streets and highways even if they did have some fuel left in the tank. Shattered glass and spilled produce littered the floor, evidence of the panicked raids that had taken place in the early days, and he crunched his way across them, aware he was making too much noise but unable to find a clear path to the back where the restroom was located. He stopped halfway, pausing to see if his presence had attracted any attention. Silence.

He moved on and pushed open the restroom door. It groaned on hinges stiff from lack of use and Zach entered. The small corridor was pitch black as the door swung closed behind him and he scrambled for his flashlight, sighing in relief as the beam showed the corridor still empty. Locating the door to the men's room, he was more prepared, removing one of his guns and readying it. With both hands occupied, he pushed the door open with his shoulder, almost expecting a screaming, snarling face to appear the moment it opened. He had created the image so clearly in his mind he was almost surprised when nothing happened. The room itself had high windows which provided natural light from the rising sun so he clicked off his flashlight and tucked it safely back into his pocket. One by one, he checked the stalls, not wishing to be taken by surprise while he was otherwise occupied. The room was clear.

Zach was relieved to step back outside, buildings held no sense of safety or security any more. Instead, they provided too many places to hide, too many dark, shadowy areas where danger could lurk undetected or where you could end up cornered and trapped, the safe haven becoming a tomb. He gave an involuntary shiver, recalling the early days when screams of rage and terror, both human and inhuman, were all that could be heard from wherever you tried to hide. He was still incredulous that he and most of his team, all scientists focused on their research, distracted and not even equipped to live in the real world, had made it through this. He removed his helmet and retrieved a bottle of water from the pannier, leaning against the bike as he took a big swig, still contemplating his own dumb luck. He couldn't help but wonder if the survivors, himself included, had got too cocky, too confident of their success. Suddenly, from the corner of his eye, he thought he spotted movement.

Zach turned quickly and saw the figure of a male in the distance. The man too had stopped in his tracks on spotting Zach and for a second, they stared at one another. The figure was large, almost six foot tall, broad at the shoulders and from what Zach could make out, was dressed in army fatigues. As it didn't scream and make its way towards him, Zach figured it was somebody from the Zone out on a routine patrol, but the way he was staring made Zach nervous. He raised his hand in a wave of greeting and his movement broke the spell between them. Zach's water bottle fell from his hand as the man turned to run, and gave away the uneven, clumsy, loping gait of a zombie.

Zach immediately gave chase, cursing himself for having the rifle jammed along the side of the bike, unready to fire, and for all the guns having their safeties on. He had taken too many precautions and now they slowed him down as he fumbled with one of the hand guns as he ran. The creature had disappeared around a corner, and as Zach skidded round the same one, he came to a halt. The street was empty. He examined the buildings on either side, all apartment blocks by the looks of it. It could be inside waiting in any one. Zach took several steps down the street, careful to stick to the middle of the road. Up ahead, he could see a dead end, explaining why the road was devoid of abandoned vehicles, only a few parked cars sat at the side of the road in allocated parking bays. It had to have ducked inside a building on this street, the wall at the end was too high and smooth to scale. He gave himself time to wonder at the intelligence of that move. Perhaps he was mistaken? Maybe this was just a man surviving out here on his own. An injury could have caused the awkward gait and Zach hadn't really been close enough to tell one way or another.

"Hello," he called out. "Is anyone there? I'm not looking to hurt anyone, I'm hunting a creature, not a person."

Other than his voice echoing, there was no reply. It occurred to Zach that this person might be the drifter who'd shot and killed Tom Smith. If that was the case, Zach was a sitting duck out here. He didn't carry food, but his weapons and bike would certainly be worth killing for. He moved closer in towards the parked cars, hoping they would give some cover if anyone opened fire on him. He continued to move down the street, slowly, turning every few steps to ensure he kept an eye on every approach, glancing up at windows as he did so. He slowed as he came upon a car with the sidewalk side doors and trunk partially open.

He tried to peer into the car as he approached but his vision was obstructed by the sun glinting off the windshield. He reached the hood, sliding his way along the side of the car, both hands gripping the handle of the gun. He could see now that the front was empty and the back seats appeared that way too. Didn't mean to say someone wasn't hiding on the floor in the back. He move further forward, allowing himself a better view. The car was empty. He took a deep breath and steeled himself to check the trunk. Once again, an image filled his mind, a man hiding there, on his back, gun at the ready, Zach's face blown to smithereens by repeated shots the minute he stepped round and raised the trunk. He pushed it away and moved fast, intending to fire the first shot. His plan might have worked, but he was left staring at the bullet hole through the bottom of the empty trunk, the sound of his shot ringing in his ears, blocking out the sound of the door to his right opening. The next thing he knew, something slammed into him, sending him flying into the middle of the road where he stumbled and fell.

Chapter Five

Face down on the ground, Zach heard the inhuman, guttural scream and he scrambled to turn around to face his assailant. His leathers had saved him from any injury during the fall, but he'd lost his grip on the gun, which had skittered across the road out of his reach. He didn't have time to retrieve another as the creature was almost upon him. As Zach stared at the hollow, almost skeletal face, the dripping, slavering jaws and the tattered army clothing, he was left in no doubt what he was facing this time. He felt frozen, like a rabbit in headlights as it lumbered towards him, favoring its left leg.

Breaking his fear-induced paralysis, Zach bent both knees and waited, using every inch of his inner resolve not to attempt to get to his feet in the few nanoseconds he had before it reached him. Poised, he waited. As the creature reached and bent forward with its anxious maw, Zach kicked as hard as he could, landing his heavy boots dead center on the monster's chest, sending it staggering backwards, flailing its arms to keep its balance. Zach got up and advanced, the zombie meeting his attack head on, showing an inordinate amount of strength as they grappled, Zach attempting to bring the creature to its knees. The creature attempted to get at his face, the only exposed part of his body, his leathers protecting him from the long, ugly scratching talons and the snapping jaw as they fought and punched.

Finally, Zach managed to take advantage of the weaker leg, another hefty kick to the knee dropping the half man, half animal. Zach quickly applied the handcuffs provided to him by Pete before he set out, intending to retrieve them after the deed was done. The creature knelt there, head down, arms behind its back, silent, as if it already knew what fate awaited it. Zach stood in front of it as he removed the second handgun from his hip holster. The metallic snaps and clicks of him preparing the gun to fire echoed back from the empty buildings around them. He raised his arm, carefully aiming the gun at the bent head in front of him, taking his time in hopes of a quick, clean kill.

"Don't."

Zach stared, hardly able to believe what he thought he had just heard, his expression almost comically incredulous. "What? Did you just ... *say* something?"

"Please ... don't ...shoot."

The voice was hoarse and cracked, like an old man left abandoned in a neglectful nursing home that'd had no occasion to use it for many years, the words uncertain, hesitant. This was impossible! The basic level of brain activity that remained after the virus had wreaked its havoc was not enough for speech. He had seen some of the older ones communicate only with uncoordinated touches and basic grunts, and he'd had no reason to believe it would ever advance beyond this. Scientific curiosity overcame him, and he studied the creature more closely. Judging by the clothes and the state of the body, it wasn't old, had only turned a month or two ago at most, there was no way it should have regained this level of intelligence so fast. Despite feeling ridiculous, he spoke in return.

"Why shouldn't I?"

The creature raised its head and Zach gasped. Yes, the hollow face and dripping jaws screamed monster, but the eyes! They weren't the usual empty, staring voids of nothingness he'd come to expect. They were dark brown, and in them, he could read emotions, anger, sorrow, despair, he saw them all flicker within. Slowly, the gun began to drop.

"Help me," it pleaded, the words barely formed around the swollen, blackish tongue.

"What are you?" Zach asked, more to himself than anyone else, not really expecting an answer.

"Infected."

Zach put his gun away and knelt down on the ground beside the creature. It shrank away.

"Too close, can't stop."

Zach backed up a little. "Are you telling me that you don't want to hurt me but you can't help yourself? That the urge is to strong."

The creature nodded and turned it's large, dark eyes upon him, pleading and longing at the same time.

"Do you remember how you were infected?"

"Remember … everything."

Dear God! Zach struggled to get his head around the possibility, how it would feel to remember everything about you that was human and right, yet be trapped inside a body that craved to rip and tear at human flesh, the urges too great to ignore. This man was in a special kind of hell and part of Zach told him to put the thing out of its misery, but the scientist in him couldn't listen. This was something different. For some reason, the virus hadn't eradicated the man inside, and he needed to know why.

"Listen to me, I can try to help you, but you need to help me. I need to take you back to my lab. I need to study you, your brain, your blood, your tissue. I'm trying to find a cure, will you come back with me?"

"Bite."

"Yeah, okay, I get it. You'll bite me at any opportunity. Guess the bike's out of the question then."

Zach looked around, wondering what to do. He wished he'd decided to carry the walkie talkie with him and not leave it with the bike, but he hadn't really anticipated a use for it other than if he needed to report in for a team to come and kill him before he turned. There was no one in sight that could help, and even if there were, he would be reluctant to enlist their services. They would want to kill this thing in front of him straight away, seeing only one of the abominations that had almost wiped out civilization, not understanding the importance it might have. His team were the only ones who could be trusted. Zach had no choice but to get back to the bike and retrieve the walkie talkie. He turned to the kneeling zombie.

"Wait here, I'll be back in a sec."

With no reason to believe the creature would obey, Zach sprinted back to where he had left the bike. He grabbed the radio and turned it on, calling back to Zone 3 base and putting in a request for them to get Mike to contact him on a certain frequency. He left the radio on, its volume turned to high, and slipped it inside his top pocket. Spotting his motorcycle helmet sitting on the seat where he had left it, he snatched it up before racing back to the spot he had left the zombie. To his great relief, it was still there, kneeling in the middle of the road. Zach rushed up behind it, slamming the full-faced helmet on over its head and buckling it tightly under the chin. It didn't even try to fight and seemed to gladly accept Zach's help to get to its feet. With its mouth covered and hands still cuffed behind its back, Zach began the long walk back to Zone 1, hoping the call from Mike would come soon. Just because the creature was docile right now didn't mean it would remain that way. Perhaps the human side was in charge right now, and that could shift at any moment. As unprecedented as this way, there was no way to tell. He'd already had a taste of how strong it was, if it chose to fight, he'd given it a weapon and protection by putting the helmet on.

They'd been walking for about thirty minutes when the radio sparked to life inside his pocket. He paused, letting go of the hold he had on the cuff chain to answer it.

"Mike, I'm at the crossroads of," Zach glanced around, looking for street signs. "Jefferson Avenue and Lincoln Drive. Can you plot a route to get a car through to pick me up? I've got a live one I need to bring in."

"Sure," the voice crackled on the other end. "I'll get the army boys out to you."

"No, no army, not this time. You know they hate me keeping the things alive. Any resistance and they'll shoot to kill, and I really need this one."

"Fine, but it might take me a while to get to you. I don't know the roads like those boys."

"That's okay, we'll head along Jefferson and keep moving west, just find us as soon as possible."

"Will do. Be careful."

Zach tucked the radio away and carried on walking. An hour later, he'd never been more relieved to hear the sound of an engine in his life.

Chapter Six

The journey passed without incident, except for Mike's pure disbelief at what Zach had found. Unwilling to make the back seat passenger act like a performing monkey, he'd refrained from conversing with it just to prove himself right for Mike's benefit. He would see soon enough. As they pulled up as close to the entrance of the underground facility as they could, Zach wondered if he should have blindfolded the creature as an extra precaution, just in case it should escape. Figuring he was too late, the two men went ahead with the transfer.

Suddenly, the thing decided it'd had enough and both were thankful for not only the motorcycle helmet they'd left in place, but also the army personal who heard the guttural screams from below and came running to assist. It took four of them and the scientists to get the enraged zombie into a cell and sedated.

"This one should be eradicated immediately, it's too strong," the one in charge declared, glowering at Zach.

"It's caged now, its fine. Thanks for your help, we can take it from here."

With one last uncertain look, the military personnel left the two men alone with the zombie. Zach had taken the precaution of placing it alone, unsure of how the others would react to it. He was afraid they would recognize it as different from them and attack it.

"There's no way that thing spoke to you, you must have been hallucinating. Lack of sleep, dehydration…"

"I know what it looks like, Mike, but how do you think I managed to get it restrained and the helmet on if it didn't let me? You've seen how strong he is."

"Oh, so it's a he now? Zach, you're losing the plot."

"Just please trust me and help me out here. The army personnel are already making noises about not keeping him, that he's too strong to be safe. If they get any inkling as to how intelligent it is, I won't be able to reason with them. Stay with him, and when he comes round, tell him to keep it hidden except from you and me, okay?"

"Sure, I'll sit and chat with the flesh eating zombie, no problem."

Mike was disgruntled and still disbelieving, but Zach knew he'd come around once he saw what he'd seen, and he knew he'd do as he'd been asked. Secure in the knowledge that his new acquisition was safe for the moment, he headed into his lab with the blood he had drawn from him once the sedation had taken effect. Putting a drop on a slide, he inserted into the same type of machine he's used and left behind at Zone 3 the day before. He waited impatiently for the results to collate, then watched in amazement as for the first time the machine let him down. The read out on the display screen was going haywire, unable to settle on any figures, the numbers changing every few seconds until they became such a blur, Zach could no longer read them.

"Must be faulty," he muttered, whishing he hadn't left the other one behind.

He placed another drop of blood on a fresh slide and slid it under his microscope. Focusing the delicate piece of equipment, he couldn't quite believe what he was seeing. On the slide, a war was raging. Healthy, human cells were under attack from ones already affected by the virus, but just as fast, the normal cells were fighting back, almost eradicating the virus completely before being overcome once again. The man's entire bloodstream must be a mass of constantly changing and adapting cells.

"No wonder the machine went nuts!" Zach murmured, his thoughts already racing as to how to identify what this man's blood contained that allowed it to fight the infection. If he could pinpoint it and enhance it, he was not only well on the way to finding a cure, but he could also create a vaccine for immunity against the virus. As long as he had a supply of this man's blood long enough to figure it all out, he could ensure the survival of the human race and prevent this ever happening again.

Jubilant, he dashed from the lab, hardly able to contain himself, desperate to share the news with Mike and get him working on it with him straight away. He didn't pause when he heard the half-human scream echoing in the corridors, he was used to that. When the following rally of gunshots rang out in response, Zach stopped in his tracks. Mike came down the corridor with an apologetic look on his face, a deep scratch down his left cheek.

"I'm sorry," Mike said. "I'm so sorry. He spoke to me Zach, he actually spoke! Intelligent conversation. My God! I couldn't believe it. I let my guard down, Zach, I got too close. I've let you down."

An armed army officer stepped round the corner, his weapon aimed at Mike. He spoke into a radio clipped to his shirt. "Subject one neutralized, subject two in my sights."

Zach dropped to his knees and sobbed.

THE END

OUR LIVING FUNERAL

CHELSEY BAKER

The heavy, beige colored subway doors closed with a definitive thud. Riley sat perfectly still in her seat, feeling the momentum of the train move her body as it slowly picked up speed again, careening down the track she couldn't see. Her green eyes wandered until she could see her mother's shoulders in her periphery, mere inches away from her own. Nancy had on a floral blouse with cut out shoulders. Riley could see her mother's tan skin slightly sway as the subway rushed forward under the Chicago streets. Since the divorce, Riley's mother had begun to dress like a woman half her age.

Nancy stared down at the grungy brown floor of the train. All she could see was a myriad of shoes and a piece of foil from a gum wrapper. She wiggled her feet, watching the overhead light shine off of her red toenails. Her eyes wandered to her daughter's shoes beside her. She wore dingy black Chuck Taylors. A hole had begun to form near one of the soles.

"You need new shoes," Nancy said quietly.

Riley glanced down at her feet. "These are fine," she replied.

"Fine? There's a hole in your right one."

Riley sighed, staring at the fake happy people that smiled down at her from the advertisements that lined the ceiling of the train car. There were so many things, a litany of things, she could argue with her mother about. Her shoes felt too easy as the subject.

"I'll get new ones, alright?" Riley said and scratched her cropped brown hair.

Nancy hated when Riley moved her arms about. She always tried to look away, but it felt as though her eyes were magnetic and couldn't help but stare at the crooks of her daughter's elbows. A series of red sores and bruises covered her daughter's pale, sallow looking skin. Most had scabbed over but they still looked angry, defiant almost. It felt as though each little sore looked back at Nancy, mocking her.

"You didn't have a long sleeved shirt to wear?"

Riley turned her neck to look at her mother. Her light brown eyes were steely as she gazed back. Fine lines surrounded the corners of Nancy's lips. Riley had the same slightly upturned nose as her mother, but it was the only thing that looked familiar. It was the only thing they shared.

"I'm sorry that my addiction embarrasses you," Riley snapped through gritted teeth.

She didn't bother to keep her voice down. An elderly man with thick round glasses glanced at her before blinking and turning his head away.

It had only been four hours since Riley had been kicked out of the Gateway Alcohol and Drug Treatment Center, but she absorbed her mother's shame as though it were her favorite sweater. It was familiar.

"I'm not embarrassed," Nancy snapped, running a hand through her shoulder length brown hair. "I just... Don't like to see what you've done to your body."

Silence reigned. Mother and daughter listened as the train clicked and whirred along the track. Their bodies swayed slightly as the subway shifted upward, barreling up from underground towards Belmont. Riley watched as trees suddenly appeared on either side of the murky windows, brown and green blurs that lined the two story brownstones, built in rows along the track.

Her thoughts meandered to Gateway, and the way the woman at the front desk looked at her as she was being escorted out by security. She pictured the joint, all wrinkled and burnt, that her counselor had found in her room. It was just to take the edge off—the dive and plummet of withdrawal that had her body in a vice grip. But all they had seen was a rule broken.

Nancy sighed, feeling the subtle ache of a headache begin to form in the center of her forehead. Her thoughts were also on Gateway, and the conversation she had with Tim before she had driven to pick up her daughter.

"Jesus, she got kicked out again?" her ex-husband had complained on the phone. "How could you let this happen?"

She had hung up on him, but his words clung to the air around her like smoke. How could you let this happen? They were divorced and Riley's addiction to heroin still caused them to argue. It felt like their marriage had died the moment their daughter put a needle to her flesh.

Nancy rubbed her temples, glancing at the people around them. The man with the thick glasses that sat across from them had dozed off, his head tilted back against the wall. A heavy set woman with bushy blonde hair read a romance novel beside him. To the right was a middle aged Asian man frowning as he stared down at his phone.

A cough rang out. Nancy followed the sound to the other side of the train, where a balding man sat in the corner. His skin was pasty and slightly shiny with sweat. He sat hunched in a dark green jacket, gazing at the floor.

Nancy's stomach lurched and she forced herself to look away. The man looked how Riley did whenever she stopped using. Those days where her daughter shivered and said she was ready to be done with heroin for good. How many times had those words left her lips? How many times did Nancy have to endure hearing them, knowing they were false?

The train began to slow as it approached a stop. The dozing man opened his eyes, and got to his feet with a soft groan. The woman with the romance novel glanced up at him as she turned a page. The heavy subway doors slid open and the man trudged off. A young woman with a purple backpack walked onto the train, her tennis shoes squeaking slightly as she turned left and sat in an empty seat across from the coughing man.

The doors came to a close, and everyone leaned to the right as the train began to move. Riley felt her stomach drop slightly as the tracks began to dip down, hurling underground again. The train grew darker as it sunk into a tunnel.

The sickly looking man began to cough again, his body heaving with the effort. Nancy found herself unable to take her eyes off him. It wasn't just the germs he spread with his incessant coughing, there was something about his eyes that looked strange, though she couldn't quite put her finger on it.

As she watched him, the man slowly rose unsteadily to his feet. His eyes were dazed as he stared at the sticky brown floor of the L train. He opened his mouth and a low, almost guttural sound emanated from his pale lips.

"What the—" Riley began when the man suddenly turned to his right and lunged at the young woman with the purple backpack.

The woman stared up in horror as the man opened his mouth wide and bit into her neck with a sickening, sepulchral noise. He tore into her flesh. Nancy and Riley watched in horror and leapt from their seats, as the other train goers cried out and screamed. There were eight people total, including the sick man. All of them flew over seats and down the aisle way.

All but one.

The heavy set blonde woman trembled in her seat, her brown eyes wide with shock as she watched the sick man continue to devour the young woman. Her hazel eyes were turned toward the ceiling, but they could no longer see.

Riley and her mother stood with the others on the opposite side of the train. There were five of them total. The middle aged Asian man who had been on his phone clutched at his heart through his shirt, breathing heavily. A teenaged girl cried in the corner, her heavy black eyeliner ran down her face. Between the two was a muscular black man with a gold earring. Riley stared at the blonde woman, her fingers still clutching the pages of her romance novel in her seat.

"MOVE!" Riley bellowed.

Her voice was loud and frantic. The sick man looked up from the young woman's corpse, his face covered in her blood. His eyes, which seemed to have turned slightly yellow, shifted from Riley to the blonde lady. He growled, shoving the dead woman aside as though she were a rag doll, and stood upright. His gaze seemed hazy and unfocused. Nancy got the distinct impression that the man, whoever he was, was no longer fully there. His movements were clumsy, uncoordinated, and his expression was vacant. She wondered if he had lost all cognitive function.

The passengers on the train watched as the sick man charge forward just as the blonde woman did. She tossed herself from her seat, but her heavy body made her slow. The sick man squealed and jumped onto the woman's back.

She cried out as her legs buckled underneath his weight. Before her head hit the ground, he had already dug his teeth into the side of her neck. Blood gushed onto the floor of the train as he made contact with her carotid artery.

"No!" shrieked the teen, frantically shaking her head. Her dyed black hair flew about her face as she stared at the growing pool of blood on the floor.

"Quiet!" the black man snapped, glaring at her. "You'll attract its attention."

"Oh," Riley said and pushed between the two. Behind them was a metal door with a square window in the center. Below the window, in bold red letters read STOP DO NOT OPEN EMERGENCY USE ONLY.

Riley grabbed the silver handle and jerked it to the left, hearing the gears shift. She opened the door and waved at her mother and the others. "Into the next car!" she urged.

The Asian man was the first to run through, followed by the black man. He had grabbed the teenager's hand and pulled her after him. Nancy looked at her daughter with an appalled expression, then walked over the threshold.

The next car only had two people in it. One was a red haired man with clusters of freckles all over his face. He immediately stood up, watching as everyone piled in with a bemused expression. The other passenger was a middle aged woman with beautiful olive toned skin.

"What the hell is going on?" the red haired man demanded, looking at each of them.

"We don't know, this man just started attacking people!" the teenaged girl blubbered. She touched the metal spikes on her choker nervously.

"It's alright," the black man said, staring into their former car through the window. "The door is locked; he can't get to us."

Nancy stepped around the group and walked to the right wall of the train. Halfway up was a metal box that jutted out from the wall. On the left side was a speaker and a small silver button. "I'm gonna call the conductor," she said, and pressed the button down with her index finger.

"Hello?" Nancy said into the speaker. "There is an emergency! A man is attacking people! The police need to be called!"

Her request was met with a few moments of static and then nothing.

"Hello?!" she yelled. "Can anybody fucking hear me?!"

The teenager sobbed and sank into a seat. The Asian man sat beside her, blinking over and over again. Riley wondered if he was in shock.

"Is anybody getting service?" the black man asked, frowning down at the phone in his hand.

One by one each Chicagoan whipped out their phones and shook their heads. There were many sections of the L where nobody got service. They were underground, beneath several layers of metal and concrete.

"What do we do? What do we do?" the teenager asked, her pale, skinny body trembling.

"We should keep moving," the Asian man said, his voice soft but certain. "We should put as much distance between us and that man as humanly possible."

The black man shook his head, absentmindedly touching his moustache. "I disagree. I think we should stay here and make sure that the man doesn't go anywhere or hurts anyone else," he reasoned. "He could easily go through the other emergency door the opposite way."

The olive skinned woman quietly came forward to stand with the others. "You say he has hurt people?" she said with an accent Riley could not quite place.

"Not just hurt, he killed them!" the gothic teen said as black makeup continued to cascade down her face.

"Perhaps we should kill him? It'd be self-defense," the foreign woman reasoned, shrugging her shoulders. She wore a quartz necklace that made a soft tinkling sound as she moved.

"Whoa, whoa, whoa, I'm not killing anyone!" said the red haired man, jabbing his thumb into his mustard colored sweater. "For all I know you guys are the crazy ones!"

The black man took a step forward, glaring into his face. "All you need to do is look through that god damn window to know we aren't crazy," he snarled.

"Get out of my face!" the red haired man barked and pushed his palms against the man's chest.

Within seconds, the black man grabbed him by the collar of his sweater and shoved him. Surprised, the red haired man stumbled backwards, tripping on his own feet. His body fell into the emergency door, his head making contact with the window with a sharp crack.

Nancy flung herself between the two of them with her arms stretched out and her palms up. "Hey!" she snapped angrily. "Attacking each other is going to get us nowhere!"

The red haired man rubbed at the back of his head, a scowl on his face. The black man took a deep breath then looked down at Nancy with a curt nod.

"Okay," he said, breathing out. "Okay."

Riley ran a hand through her cropped brown hair, trying desperately not to think about getting high. Such a situation would tempt any addict, she was sure.

"Maybe we should move to the next car?" she suggested. "I doubt all of the intercoms are broken, and if we can contact the conductor, he can reach out to the police."

The Asian man nodded his head vigorously in agreement, but the black man frowned down at the ground.

"I think if we were to keep moving, panic would spread. You saw what happened to that woman when she was paralyzed with fear," he reasoned, crossing his arms across his muscular chest. "I think as long as we know where the man is, we should remain here."

"I don't want to die...," murmured the teen girl, her black hair falling around her face as she stared mournfully into her lap.

"Nobody else is fucking dying, alright?" Riley growled. "That man, whatever happened to him, looks messed up in the head."

"Well, obviously—"the black man interjected.

"No, I meant that he doesn't seem to be high functioning anymore," Riley said, cutting him off. "I don't know what happened, but I think the cognitive parts of his brain aren't working."

Nancy blinked at Riley, surprised to hear her very own thoughts come out of her daughter's mouth.

"I agree," Nancy murmured—which made Riley look surprised in turn.

"Well, that's great and all, but what are we going to do?" snapped the freckled man.

Suddenly, the emergency door on the opposite side of the train was opened and a blonde man, who appeared to be in his forties, poked his head into the car.

"Everything alright?" he asked. "We've been hearing a lot of yelling," he pointed behind him with his thumb.

The Asian man shook his head while the teen visibly shivered.

"No, man," said the black man with a grimace. "A man has started attacking and eating people. We have him isolated in the next car. Seems to be some kind of virus or infection."

The blonde man blinked at him. Riley could see his Adam's apple bob nervously above his teal colored necktie. "He's…. eating people?" he repeated, just barely above a whisper.

"Yes," Nancy nodded. "And we've been trying to contact—"

But the blonde man had shut the door with a definitive slam. Riley and Nancy watched, their jaws flying open, as the man locked the door behind him. He continued to look through the window, his expression a mixture of sorrow and resolve.

"Hey!" the black man growled, reaching the door in a couple of strides. He pounded his fist against the wall, staring at the blonde man as if he could kill him with his eyes.

"Open the door!" he demanded.

The blonde man stared back, his mouth turned down at the corners. He slowly shook his head. "I'm sorry," he mouthed. "Not safe."

The teen stared at the man from his seat, her blue eyes wide with fear. "Oh my god, we're gonna die!" she wailed and began to cry with renewed fury.

Hesitantly, the Asian man slowly moved his arm around the girl's shoulder, patting her awkwardly. To his surprise, she turned into his embrace, resting her head into the crook of his neck.

"Hopefully they contact the conductor in that car," Riley said, still staring at the blonde man. He had the decency to look sheepish as they made eye contact.

The black man slammed his fist against the door again, then turned his back to it. He sat down in the nearest seat and rested his elbows on his legs. He shook his head over and over again.

Nancy sighed, trying to suppress the rising panic she felt deep in her gut. "Okay," she said to herself. "Okay, let's think..."

She began to pace in a small circle on the brown floor of the train. Everyone was quiet apart from the teen, who continued to sob into the Asian man's shoulder.

The red haired man, who had been leaning against the wall with his arms crossed, suddenly lifted an index finger. "What if we pull the emergency brake? The conductor will instantly be notified that something is wrong," he said.

Riley shook her head, scratching at her skin. "The emergency brake should only be pulled when we are beside a platform," she argued. "If we pull the brake now, we will be stuck in this tunnel and police won't be able to reach us."

Nancy frowned up at the ceiling. Above the sound of the teenager's sobs, she heard a faint tinkling sound, like the first sprinkling of rain on a window. The train was still underground, enveloped in a tunnel of concrete.

The teen opened her mouth to speak, but Nancy shushed her, holding her hand up in the air. "Hold on," she said. "Do you guys hear that noise? What is that?"

Everyone sat still, their eyes unfocused as they concentrated on the sound.

"Where is that coming from?" Riley asked, looking out the window behind her.

Within seconds the noise became louder. Nancy and the other passengers watched in horror as pieces of glass fell from the cracked window of the emergency window. The sick man had somehow realized that the window had been broken, and was trying to crawl through.

"Ahh!" the Asian man cried and stood up from his seat. He grabbed onto the teen's black lacy shirt and pulled her with him towards the other end of the car as she screamed.

Within seconds, the black man was back on his feet, frantically rapping his knuckles against the emergency door the blonde man had gone through. "Open up!" he cried. "The man is coming in, open up!"

The passengers of the train looked at him and then to the blonde man. He sat in the first seat beside the emergency door, adjusting the collar of his shirt nervously. He was shaking his head, speaking to his fellow passengers. None of them looked happy, but they each nodded their heads, keeping their gaze down at the ceiling.

They weren't willing to risk their own lives to save anyone else.

"What do we do? What do we do?" asked the olive skinned woman, clutching at the seat in front of her with white knuckles.

"I...I'll try to take care of it," said the red haired man. He fished into the pocket of his jeans and pulled out a Swiss army knife.

The sick man had already burrowed through the window, seemingly not concerned that shards of glass were digging into his skin as he crawled through and fell to the floor head first. He growled and stood up again, looking at the passengers of the train with a hungry look in his eyes.

The red haired man clutched at his small knife and took a deep breath. With a noise of resolve, he ran forward, raising the knife up high above his head in a striking motion.

The freckled man sunk the knife deep into the man's neck as he bent forward, sinking his teeth into his forearm. Blood began to spurt from the knife wound, but the sick man still didn't seem to notice. He used the weight of his body to pull the red haired man down the ground. Hearing the man's screams made bile rise in Riley's throat.

Nancy took the steps to go from one side of the train to the other, hovering beside the black man. "You're the strongest one here, do you think you can break one of the side windows with your feet? We could get onto the roof!"

The man nodded and turned, raising his right black boot towards his waist. He gritted his teeth together as he kicked out against the glass over and over again.

"Oh god," the teenaged girl said, watching the red haired man scream and struggle against the sick man's mouth. She bent over and vomited on the floor at her feet.

Riley stared at the knife, which still protruded from the sick man's neck as he continued to attack the freckled man. "Everyone, pull out anything and everything in your pockets and bags that could be used as a weapon" she ordered.

Nancy looked down at her purse, surprised to see that it was still securely on her shoulders. She dug into the soft brown leather, feeling around until her fingers felt the long metal nail file she always kept in there.

The goth teen took off her spiked collar and wrapped it around her fingers so the spikes faced outward.

Riley had never liked purses, and typically carried her ID and phone in her jeans. She felt the outsides of her pockets, but the only thing she had on her person was a blue Bic lighter.

The overhead lights shut off as the passengers continued to search through their belongings. There were small yellow colored lights every few feet in the tunnel, but the car was mostly dark.

Nancy peered through the darkness, watching as the sick man continue to ingest the freckled man. His victim had stopped moving and making noise...

She let out a noise of despair and turned her attention back to the black man, who grunted as he thrust his boot against the window over and over again.

"Hurry!" she begged him, frantically waving her arms.

"I am!" he growled and thrust his foot against the window. The glass finally gave way. It broke into several pieces, some of which fell into the train while others fell out onto the tunnel. Riley could hear some of the shards crunch underneath the tracks of the train cars.

"Okay," she told herself and ran to where her mother stood. With deft fingers she snatched the nail file out of her mother's hand and held it as though it were a knife.

"Help everyone through the window," Riley yelled to her. "I'll take the rear."

Nancy shook her head, staring at her daughter by the faint yellow glow. "Absolutely not," she said.

"There's no time to argue, just do it!" Riley screamed back. She waved at everyone toward the very back of the car.

The black man was already halfway through the window, slowly raising his body up, careful not to scrape himself against the rough cement walls of the subway.

The Asian man helped keep the teen steady as they stood in front of the broken window. The woman with the olive toned skin had her hands out by the frame, prepared to help the black man in case he lost his balance. Nancy watched as his torso disappeared, then his thighs. All that was left on the frame were his worn black boots.

"Once I get up there, I will reach down and help everyone up!" he bellowed to the passengers below him.

He laid his body flat against the metal frame of the L train. The roof had thin grooves etched into the metal, but they weren't deep enough for the man to hold onto. He stared down the tunnel, trying to grip the train as it began to go around a sharp bend. Despite his strength, he could not find a good handhold on the metal.

"Shiiiiiiiit!" he cried, as his body began to slip sideways. He dug his fingernails into the metal but they were sweaty and betrayed him.

Nancy, Riley, and the other passengers stared in terror as the watched the black man's boots reappear, dangling from the roof of the train. They all tried to reach out for him, but the train swiftly turned, and his body moved with the momentum.

With one last agonizing cry, the black man lost his grip entirely and flew through the air. Gravity pulled him down until he tumbled onto the tracks...and was pulverized underneath the car that immediately followed.

"NOOO!" the teenaged girl shrieked, shaking her fists into the air as fresh tears careened down her pale cheeks.

"Oh my god," Nancy murmured as she poked her head out of the broken window. Blood was smeared along the bottom of the next car. Her stomach lurched and she forced herself to look away.

Inside the train, the sick man seemed to be tiring of his meal. Riley stared at his face, studying the way his eyes continued to yellow, and his skin seemed to go grey. "Guys, I think he's turning into a zombie," she murmured.

The Asian man gawked at her from beside the window. "Impossible," he said. "Zombies do not exist."

Riley watched as the sick man licked at the puddle of blood that had grown underneath the freckled man's body. "I think they do now," she said.

The woman with the olive toned skin walked to the nearest seat and set her black purse down. She rifled through it until she said "Aha!" and pulled out a crumpled piece of paper and a pen. In capital letters she wrote INFECTED MAN, PEOPLE DYING, PLEASE LET US IN. Once she was done, she tossed the pen over her shoulder and marched to the emergency door.

"Hey!" she yelled, and slammed the piece of paper against the window.

Nancy could make out a few people on the train from where she stood. The blonde man continued to sit in the chair closest to the door. He read the sign and swallowed again. Someone must have said something behind him because he turned in his chair and moved his arms about as though he were arguing.

The passengers watched as the pedestrians of the other car gestured wildly, and debated. Riley felt dread creep up her body from the tips of her toes as she tried to read their lips. If it had been her, she would have been at that door in the span of two seconds, cranking it open, saving lives.

It seemed that some people on the train felt the very same. They pointed at the sign, visible tears in their eyes as they yelled at the man in the suit.

After a few minutes of this, the blonde man moved his arms up and down as if to calm everyone. He spoke for a few minutes and then people began to raise their hands.

They were voting.

Nancy tried to count the hands, but it hardly mattered. She couldn't tell which hands voted for what. What was sickening was how close both rounds seemed to be...

The blonde man finished counting and nodded his head. He reached into the pocket of his dark grey suit and pulled out his cell phone. He worked his fingers on the screen then brought the phone over to the window. He had it open to a text message which read, SORRY U GUYS COULD BE CONTAGIOUS TOO. MORE DEATH.

The teen lurched forward and vomited again, splattering her shiny black Doc Martens.

Fed up, Riley walked to the door. She stared at the blonde man, wishing—not for the first time in her life—that she could set fire by sheer will alone. His mouth was grim, but his eyes were guarded, almost steely as he looked back.

He did not want this to happen to them. But he was not willing to risk his own life to save anyone else's, either.

Riley slowly raised both hands and stuck her middle fingers up. If she was going to die, she was going to die without whimpering.

She was going to die fighting.

Suddenly, her mother was beside her, pulling her arms back down. Riley was about to snarl at her, but she looked up at Nancy's face and knew her mother wasn't trying to chastise her. Nancy's eyes were wide but steady as she looked down at her daughter.

"I just wanted to tell you that I love you," she murmured, gently putting a hand underneath Riley's chin.

"I... I never meant for anything like this to happen," Riley whispered back, feeling tears begin to well at the bottom of her eyes.

Nancy looked into her daughter's green eyes, and knew what she meant. She meant that she never meant to get addicted to heroin. She never meant to cause problems for her family.

She had never meant to cause any of them pain.

"I know," Nancy said, forcing her mouth into a weak smile. "I know."

A strange gurgling sound caused everyone to look at the opposite end of the train. The zombie was staring up at them from the meager remains of the red haired man—some fragments of his sweater and a pile of bloody, half eaten organs.

The zombie gurgled again. Blood oozed from the corners of his mouth, down onto his chin. His eyes were neon yellow in color, and no longer contained any semblance of human emotion in their irises.

With mechanical movements, the zombie steadily rose to his feet. His eyes trailed from one passenger to another, looking at each as though they were a dish laid out on the dinner table. He stepped through the remains of the corpse, intent on selecting his next victim.

The passengers huddled together at the other end of the train. The woman with olive skin began to pound her fists against the window, tears streaming down her cheeks as she begged them to open the door.

The teen girl whispered a prayer under her breath, her eyes closed. The Asian man stood beside her, muttering under his breath in Vietnamese.

It seemed that everyone was giving up.

Riley gritted her teeth and walked to the broken window. Carefully she grabbed the largest shard of glass she could find. It looked almost like a thunderbolt, narrowing to a sharp point at one end. She could feel its edges bite into her palm, but she just took a deep breath and gripped it all the more tightly.

She turned to look at her mother.

"I don't think we can take him on alone, but we if work together...."

Nancy sucked in a deep breath, and looked from the zombie down to the shard of glass clutched in her daughter's hand.

"No matter what, I am not getting off this train without you," Riley insisted vehemently. "Either we work together and try to kill him, or we die trying. We die together."

Nancy looked at the resolve in her daughter's eyes and felt a tear spill down her right cheek. She didn't want to die, but as she faced her potential—likely inevitable end—she was surprised to find she was not afraid. Her tears were for her daughter, for her courage, for her selflessness. She saw a layer of depth and beauty she had never noticed before, etched into the planes of her daughter's face.

At last Nancy nodded, brushing at her tears with an impatient hand. "Together," she said.

And she, too, grabbed a large shard of glass.

They resolved to flank the zombie, hoping having two people approach him would cause him to remain unsure and unfocused. Riley felt as though her heart would leap up her chest and out of her throat at any moment, it pounded so furiously.

As she stepped forward, a fraction of her brain imagined how things would have pained out if she had had heroin coursing through her veins at the time of the first attack. She would have been dead. She would have been killed and eaten and her mother would have had to have watched it all.

I'm never getting high again, she told herself.

"Where should we strike first?" Nancy asked. She tried to keep her voice steady as she walked forward.

"Let's gouge his eyes out first," Riley said. "We will have the advantage if he can't see."

She saw her mother nod in her periphery.

"On three?" Riley said, looking to her mother. She forced her mouth into a smile, one last attempt at bravado.

"On three," Nancy repeated.

"1... 2... 3!" Mother and daughter said in unison and raced forward, holding the glass high above their heads.

The zombie growled, clumsily bringing his arms forward. His sickly yellow eyes darted between both of them, seemingly unsure as to who to attack first. It was this hesitation that Riley had been banking on. She cried out as she lunged forward, and swung her arm forward. She used the momentum to gather power behind her strike and thrust the glass deep into the man's left pupil.

On the right, Nancy was doing the same thing. She wasn't as physically strong as her daughter, so she twirled in a tight circle, swinging her arm out wide to strike against the zombie. The glass sunk into his iris with a nauseating noise.

The zombie howled in pain, taking several steps backward as he frantically waved his arms about. He recognized that he was in pain, but seemed incapable of removing the glass from his eyes.

"Now, let's grab them back out and strike him!" Riley cried out. Blood ebbed from her hand as she grappled the glass, but she did not register the pain. Adrenaline coursed through every vein in her body.

Mother and daughter held onto their shards and repeatedly stabbed them into the sallow, grey flesh of the zombie's body. They struck at his heart and chest over and over again as he shrieked in agony. His stab wounds grew and spread as they worked, until it became one huge, gaping wound above his ribcage.

The zombie faltered, his bloody eyes turned toward the ceiling as he began to sway in place. Riley extended one of her black Chuck Taylor's and kicked the man until he fell to the ground. His limbs spread out half-hazardly across the brown floor, unmoving.

Nancy stared down at the zombie, her eyes wide, unable to process what had happened. Beside her, Riley fished into the back pocket of her jeans and pulled out the blue Bic lighter.

"For good measure," she said and cranked the metal wheel. She placed the flame against the man's clothing until it caught fire.

"Look! We are approaching a platform!" the teen girl said, pointing out the window to the left hand side. Sure enough, Nancy could see the platform careening ever closer.

"Hit the emergency brake!" she ordered, pointing at the red lever beside the main entry doors to the train.

The Asian man leapt forward and grabbed the lever, pulling it with both hands until it gave way.

As the train came to a screeching halt, Riley felt her mother's arms come around her in a hard embrace. Riley smiled, flinging her arms around her mother's shoulders in turn. They were together and they were alive.

END

CEMETERY THINGS

JESSICA BENN

Katie was sitting on the floor of her dorm room. Papers and books were strewn around her in an arc. So far, her junior year of college had consisted of nothing but all-nighters, energy drinks, and stress eating. Her roommate's television was blaring something about a revolutionary treatment for brain tumors. "Mia, could you turn that down please?" The racket made it hard to focus. She had already read the same sentence three times.

"Mia!" Katie yelled in frustration over the news anchors as she slammed down her chemistry book. The book's hardcover sounded like a gunshot as it struck the floor. Katie tugged her black t-shirt down as she stood up. She hooked her fingers into her belt loops and jumped a little as she wiggled her jeans higher on her hips. She stomped across the living room to Mia's bedroom. Her eyes bulged in annoyance as she glared from the doorway.

Mia had her toothbrush hanging out of her mouth. A slight, minty froth gathered at the corners of her lips. Damp hair clung to her shoulders from the shower, and the steam still lingered in the air. Mia was sitting on the edge of her bed. Her blue comforter and wet towel were in a heap on the floor. Mia's eyes were wide as she kept watching the screen. Light from the television played across her face as the scenes shifted. Katie walked over to her with an exasperated sigh and plopped down next her. The TV was looping footage of a brain cancer patient who had been undergoing the newest treatment. They called it Recusant. It was an injection that targeted the mutated tumor cells and shrank the cancer. Katie watched as the video clip showed a man whose skin was sallow and cheeks were sunken in. Her frustration melted into horror as she watched, both repulsed and fascinated at the same time. She couldn't make herself look away. The patient looked more skeleton than a man. His eyes were wide and crazed as they darted back and forth hardly blinking. The tendons in his neck threatened to snap and burst free as he strained against his hospital bed. The orderlies were trying to secure his restraints, but the man lashed out at them.

A nurse ran in to help hold him down, and the man sunk his teeth into her forearm. The footage cut off abruptly and looped back to the beginning. The pane zoomed out to show the reporter in the studio while the hospital footage continued in the top, right-hand corner.

"Nurse Lee is still in critical condition and has begun to show signs of brain damage in her prefrontal cortex. Doctors caring for the injured nurse say that this area of the brain is responsible for behavior and personality. At this time, her cortex is being monitored by regularly scheduled MRI's, but specialists say there is a steady decrease in its size. Nurse Lee and the other patients who have undergone Recusant treatments are being closely monitored." The news anchor's voice remained emotionless through the story as she transitioned nonchalantly to the weather segment.

Mia turned slowly towards Katie. Her eyes welled up, and she pulled the dangling toothbrush out of her mouth with a shaking hand. Mia's mom had been one of the first patients in the trial study for the 'revolutionary scientific breakthrough of the century.' At first, it had been going well. There were improvements. There was even hope for a full recovery, but as the doses increased, the side effects became more apparent. Now, Mia had just seen a sneak peek at what was going to happen to her mother. Katie's heart sagged as she hugged Mia tightly through her sobs.

Katie's phone started ringing in her pocket. She pulled it out and saw Kacey's face on the screen. She hadn't kept in touch very well with her little sister since school had started back up. Guilt settled in the pit of her stomach. Kacey was in high school now. She played the flute in the marching band and was on the debate team. She had texted Katie a few times this semester and asked if she could make it to her recital or come watch her debate, but Kacey had been so overwhelmed with her classes that she had never even texted back. The guilt twisted in Katie's gut as she slid her finger over to ignore the call from her little sister. She focused on rocking Mia gently. The rhythmic swaying helped to calm them both. Katie could feel warm tears seep into the shoulder of her t-shirt. Her roommate's muffled cries were punctuated with sharp inhales as Mia's body tried desperately to remind her to breathe. Katie's phone rang again. "I've gotta take this." Katie's voice was gentle and comforting, but the guilt squirmed in her stomach, "I'll be right back, ok?" She gave her roommate an extra tight squeeze and handed her the teddy bear that was laying on Mia's pillow. Mia curled up on her bed and squeezed the bear to her chest, still rocking slightly. She reached out and took the picture frame from her bedside table and ran her finger over her mom's face. The glass had a light sheen of moisture from remaining humidity in the room. Her fingertip caused the glass to squeak as it skidded along the surface. The picture was from Mia's high school graduation. She and her mother had the same dark hair and the same slender build. People had always teased them that they could be sisters, but that was before the cancer had taken hold.

"Hello," Katie half whispered into her phone, "Kace, this isn't really a good—what? Wait. Slow down. Who's doing what now?"

Kacey's voice was panicked, "Some of the patients escaped! CDC has put up roadblocks and the town is under quarantine. They're attacking people! The news said they've already had two confirmed murders, and at least five are injured. Mom's out of town on business, and dad isn't answering his phone. I'm scared, Katie. I dunno what to do." Katie could hear her sister begin to hyperventilate.

"Whoa, hold on." Katie was trying to process all of this at once. People like that guy on TV were out roaming the streets, killing people, and Kacey was home alone. "Ok," she said trying to kick herself into adult mode, "lock the door. I'll be there as soon as I can. Don't let anyone in. Promise me."

"I...I promise." Kacey's voice faltered between her quick, shallow breaths.

"I mean it, Kace. No one." Katie hung up the phone. Her thoughts were racing. She had been a crappy sister the past few months, but this was more important than her studies. When it really counted, she had to be there for Kacey. The guilt in her stomach writhed and solidified into a formidable foundation of determination. Katie let out a slow, deep breath as she allowed the situation to sink in.

"Hey, Mia," Katie walked gently back to Mia's doorway trying to remain calm for her friend's sake, "I gotta go. Kacey needs me right now...are you going to be ok? Do you want me to call someone for you? Jack, maybe?" Mia's boyfriend wasn't the best at emotional support, but at least it was something. Katie's heart thudded and drummed against her ribs, but her external, placid façade remained in place.

Mia sat up still clutching her ragged, tear-stained bear, "Would it be ok if I just came with you?" Her voice was meek, and she looked so vulnerable.

Katie looked at her and weighed the options. This could be dangerous, and Mia wasn't in the right frame of mind to deal with that right now. She wasn't in the right frame of mind to be left alone either, though. If Katie left Mia behind, she would be worried about her and wouldn't be able to focus fully on taking care of Kacey. There was a rumble outside and the sound of screeching brakes. "What the hell?" Kacey strode over to the window. Military jeeps had started to form a perimeter around the campus. "Shit. Mia, grab your crap. We have to go."

"What is it?" Mia walked up to the window and saw the insignia on one of the vehicles. "Why is the National Guard here?"

Katie grabbed her backpack and dumped its contents on the floor. "Some of the Recusant patients escaped the hospital," she said while shoving an extra hoodie and a couple bottles of water into her bag. "Kace said they were putting up quarantines. Mom is out on business, and she can't get ahold of dad." Katie paused, "Do we have any weapons?" It was such a weird question to hear herself asking.

"Weapons?" Mia looked at Katie quizzically. "We have steak knives, but that's about it. Did...did she say which patients?" Mia had followed Katie into the kitchen. "Why do you need a weapon?" Mia's second question was an afterthought. Her mind was focused almost entirely on one uncertainty: Was her mother one of the escapees?

Katie stopped rifling through the silverware drawer and looked up at her friend. Mia was pale as she clutched the edge of the counter. "No," Katie's voice was empathetic, "she didn't say any names, but some of them have ,already hurt people. I just want to be prepared. Get together some clothes and anything else you want, ok? We have to leave before they get us all blocked in. We can call the hospital when we get to my parents' house and check on your mom."

Mia nodded meekly and went to her room to pack her things. Her arms stayed still at her side as she walked, trancelike, into her bedroom. Katie went back to looking through the kitchen drawers. Spoon, spoon, fork. "Where the heck are all of our frigging knives?" She mumbled to herself. She opened the dishwasher which was packed full of dirty dishes. The smell of caked on food busted free from the opening. "You've got to be kidding me." Katie wrinkled her nose, pulled out two of the cleanest looking knives in the silverware section, and started scrubbing them in the sink.

"Remain calm. Everyone stay in your dorms." A voice echoed from a speaker outside.

"Let's go, Mia!" Katie yelled from the kitchen while she wiped the knives off on a dish rag. She slung her backpack over her shoulders and grabbed a ball cap to cover her short, messy hair. Mia came out of her room with a duffle bag strap swung across her body. Her wet hair was tied up in a ponytail. Her green shirt was darker where her hair had dripped on it, and the hems of her blue jeans were frayed. Katie handed her a knife.

"You really think we're going to need these?" Mia held the knife pinched between her middle finger and thumb like it was a dirty diaper she couldn't wait to throw away.

"I would rather have it and not need it than need it and not have it," Katie said matter-of-factly as she opened the dorm door and poked her head out into the hallway. Students were wandering to both exits trying to see what was going on outside. Katie held open the door and let Mia step into the hall before following. She turned and looked around their room before closing and locking the door behind them. The click of the lock had a ring of finality to it. Katie grabbed Mia's shoulders, turning her so that they were looking one another in the eye. "Stay close."

Mia nodded and tried to conceal her panic. The two of them shouldered past their classmates until they reached the glass door that led to the campus grounds. A crowd had already gathered. "I guess no one told the National Guard the best way to get college kids to go somewhere is to either tell them not to go there or offer them free food," Katie said under her breath while she kept an eye on the commotion. There was a soldier placed every two feet across the main entrance to the campus. They kept shifting nervously. Their posture was casual, and even from this far away Katie could tell their boots weren't up to spec. She grew up as a military brat. Her dad was a Marine, and they had lived on military bases most of her life. These weren't combat-tested soldiers, hardened and ready to kill if necessary. These poor guys had barely made it out of basic. They looked like they should be at a frat party, not lined up like a firing squad. Katie tightened her grip on her knife and kept it close to her side as she and Mia walked in the opposite direction from the crowd.

"Miss? Excuse me, miss?" One of the soldiers had spotted them.

"Keep going. Don't look back." Katie grabbed Mia's arm and pulled her along faster. They were almost off the grass. The sidewalk was only a few feet away.

"Miss!" He was approaching them with his gun firmly grasped in both hands. The barrel gleamed in the afternoon sun as he held it upright. Katie could see him out of the corner of her eye. He had dark hair, and his broad shoulders were slumped forward slightly. His long legs were closing the gap. Katie quickened her pace.

Suddenly, an ear-splitting scream cut through the air. The crowd of students started scattering, and gunshots rang out. Katie and Mia instinctively turned towards the sounds and saw three people in St. Mary's hospital gowns near the soldiers. It looked like one of the of the soldiers had tried to talk the patients into backing down, but they had lunged forward and bit him. The guardsmen were now firing at the patients. The bullets didn't seem to faze them. The patients kept chewing on him, and chunks of his flesh made sickening, wet, smacks on the sidewalk as they tore him apart. The soldier who had called out to them earlier looked torn between returning to his ranks or securing the girls. He squared his jaw and locked eyes with Katie.

He sprinted determinedly towards her just as one of the patients grabbed a freshman girl and sank her teeth into the tender flesh of the girl's shoulder. "Let's move!" he yelled at them. His booming voice jolted Katie out of her disbelief at what was happening, and she followed him as he ran past. Mia was still shocked by the massacre that was unfolding in front of the school.

"Mia!" Katie yelled over her shoulder. Mia snapped out of her trance and forced her legs to move.

The three of them ran down Main Street until they were three blocks away from the college. The further into town they got, the more disaster they saw. Bodies were strewn between the stores. Some people were still alive. Thick, sticky blood spurted with every heartbeat from a man who was clutching a gash in his thigh. A pool of blood was forming quickly around him. Those who hadn't been mauled by the Recusant patients were either trying to stem the bleeding of the living or taking this opportunity to loot for personal gain. The chaos brought out the worst in people.

Windows were smashed. Glass and fresh blood gleamed in the sunlight. Men and women fought in the streets for impractical items. A fifty-inch TV wouldn't save them from the epidemic. Liquor wouldn't fend off the attacks. Jewelry wouldn't keep their loved ones safe. They were stupid and materialistic, and they were going to die. Instead of running or securing themselves in a locked building, they were out here stealing. Katie dodged past two men carrying a sofa out of a broken storefront window. Another man ran at her and tried to grab her bag. She swung around and drove a kick into his chest. He sprawled backward looking shocked and then scrambled away. No one and nothing was going to keep her away from her little sister, not this time. Katie looked up to see the soldier looking at her surprised and slightly amused. "What?" She asked defensively.

"No, nothing. Just surprised you landed that kick is all." He said with a smirk. "Impressive. I'm Eric by the way."

"Mia."

"Katie."

"Where are you guys headed?" Eric kept checking their perimeter. "Do you know anywhere we can ride this out?"

"We're going to my parents' place over on Oak Hill Avenue. My little sister Kacey is home alone right now, and she needs me." Katie hoisted her bag higher on her shoulders and started winding her way through the bodies and the looters. Glass crunched under her sneakers.

Eric let Mia follow after her friend while he took up the rear, "My unit was called in after the police were unable to contain the situation. We were supposed to take the targets into custody. If that failed, the next order was shoot to kill. I never actually thought I would be put in that situation, though." Eric paused for a moment, lost in thought. He had only signed up for the Guard to help pay for his college. In the back of his mind, he always knew it was a possibility that he would see combat, but he never thought it would actually happen. Eric's face hardened as he thought about the decisions he made that had led up to this moment. "You live your life. You go out drinking, and you ignore the people you care about because you're too tired or too drunk to deal with their shit, you know? Then something happens that makes you take a good hard look at yourself." Eric's voice filled with self-loathing, "You know the last thing I said to my mom? I told her I was too busy hanging out with my buds, and I would call her back later. Now I'll probably never get to talk to her again. Not the real her anyway."

Katie glanced over her shoulder at him and saw his name patch. "Lee? Your last name's Lee?" She stopped walking. "Was your mom the nurse?"

Eric nodded. His mouth was a taut, thin line. His Adam's apple quivered, "Every time I close my eyes I see that news footage of her getting bitten. She wasn't even supposed to be there. She took an extra shift to cover for her coworker who wanted to go to her kid's little league game."

"My mom was a trial patient," Mia said quietly. The two of them looked at one another sharing a palpable loss that made Katie's heartache.

"We need to keep moving," Katie said as a woman on the ground started twitching. "We may not have much time."

The three of them watched as their town descended into madness. It was insane to imagine that all of these bodies were your everyday grocers, baristas, and soccer moms. "How could three people cause this much damage?" Katie asked as they passed a minivan that had crashed into a stoplight. The light was flashing red.

"They didn't." Eric was looking straight ahead. His left foot was pointing forward, and his right foot was a pace behind. He slowly lowered his gun from its upright position and aimed it at something moving on the other side of an overturned truck.

Katie backed up slowly until she was standing beside Eric. "What do we do?" She whispered while keeping her eyes on the figure that was still only partially visible.

"See the alley to your left?" Eric's voice was barely audible as he pushed his gun's safety into the off position. There was a light click as it slid into place.

"Yeah." Katie glanced towards the alleyway. Mia was still a few paces in front of them. She was shaking.

"You and Mia go that way. I'll meet you between Spruce and Sycamore Street." Eric had the gun pressed against his shoulder. His finger rested against the outside of the trigger.

Katie placed her hand lightly on Mia's arm. Mia jumped at her touch, and when she turned around silent tears trickled down her face. Katie took Mia's hand and tried to lead her down the deserted alleyway, but she wouldn't move. She just looked back towards the truck.

That's when Katie saw the person move out from behind the bed of the vehicle. She recognized the slender build, even without the dark hair.

"Mom?" Mia's voice broke and she took a step forward. Her knife clattered to the ground. Her mom's head tilted to one side and then slowly rotated to the other. "Mom!" Mia's voice was pained and breathy. She struggled against Katie's restraining hand.

"Mia, no!" Katie grabbed onto Mia's wrist with both hands and dug in her heels.

Mia's mom pulled her lips back to bare her teeth. Dried blood stained her mouth. Her hospital armband glinted in the sun, and her maroon gown fluttered in the breeze.

"Mom...mom, it's me. It's Mia. It's me!" Mia's voice pleaded across the street.

What used to be Mia's mom charged at them. Her bare feet scraped across the pavement with every step. Mia broke free from Katie's grasp and ran towards her mom. Katie fell backward landing on tiny shards of glass that still littered the sidewalk. She watched as her friend raced towards the monster her mother had become.

A single shot rang out across the street. The silence immediately following it was deafening. For a single moment, the chaos around them was completely still. The bullet had gone straight through the skull. Mia's mom staggered in mid stride. She dropped to her knees and then fell, face forward, onto the asphalt.

Mia screamed and dropped to her own knees. She started beating her legs and doubled over letting out the most primal sound Katie had ever heard. Mia began slamming her head into the pavement. The shrill keening escalated in volume as her grief mounted. Katie crawled over to her and pulled her upright. Mia tried to push her away, but Katie held her tight.

"Guys," Eric said, "there's more of them."

His voice brought him to Mia's attention. She elbowed Katie in the chest and scrambled towards him. Her grief doubled her strength. Katie grabbed her ankles, but Mia kicked her off. She got to her feet and rammed her shoulders into Eric's stomach. He staggered backward a few paces before he was able to brace himself against her attack.

"Mia, it wasn't her anymore!" Katie yelled at her. "Stop it! You saw her. That thing wasn't your mom. She had blood on her mouth, Mia. Blood. Those people at the college, the ones who started attacking the students? That is what she had become. She was one of them."

Mia turned from her attack on Eric and looked at Katie. "She was my mom." Mia's eyes were full of sorrow and desperation. She turned to look at her mom's body sprawled in the street. This was the woman who had worked three jobs to help pay for her college, the woman who had put off her chemo treatments because she thought showing up bald at a high school graduation would embarrass her daughter, the woman who had sacrificed so much for her. She didn't deserve this, to be gunned down in the middle of the street because some scientists in a lab created a horrible new drug. This wasn't fair. She had given so much of herself, and now she was just lying there. She looked so frail and helpless. Mia walked towards her mother. She didn't deserve this. That single thought consumed every part of Mia. She didn't deserve this.

There were four more patients emerging from behind vehicles. They were joined by several pedestrians that all had bloodstained clothing and irregular gashes along their arms and upper body. Eric grabbed Katie around the waist and threw her over his shoulder. He headed for the alleyway away from the approaching Recusant patients and their new victims.

"We can't just leave her!" Katie yelled at him.

"She won't come with us willingly, and right now she's more of a liability."

"But she's going to die!"

"And if we stay and try to drag her with us, so will we!" Eric started jogging towards the end of the alley.

From her position over his shoulder, Katie could see Mia kneeling by her mother. She had pulled her mom's head into her lap and was stroking her cheek. They made it around the corner of the building before Mia's screams started. Katie grabbed two fistfuls of the back of Eric's shirt and closed her eyes. After they had gone a few blocks and the screams had faded, Eric set Katie back on her feet. He leaned his gun against the nearest building. He took her face in his hands and rested his forehead on hers. "Look at me." He said. His blue eyes stared into hers. "You can grieve later. I need you to be strong right now. Do what you gotta do, ok?"

Katie stared back at him. She was having trouble breathing.

"Katie, stay with me, ok? Think about your sister. What was your sister's name? Kerry?"

"Kacey."

"Alright, you have to focus for Kacey, ok? Can you do that?" He absent-mindedly stroked her cheek with his thumb and then caught himself.

"Yeah. Yeah, I can do that." Katie steeled herself. She had to think about Kacey. She could deal with everything later. She closed her eyes and took in a deep breath. She could do this. Her eyes flew open. "Where's my knife?" She looked around and then back the way they had come. "I must have dropped it while I was trying to stop—," She couldn't say Mia's name. If she said it, it would be admitting Mia was dead, and she couldn't do that yet.

"Here." Eric pulled a knife out of his combat boot and handed it to her. "Use mine."

"Thanks." The knife was heavier than it looked. The hilt was black and ribbed to fit a man's natural grip. The steel was heavily polished and blinded her momentarily as it caught the sunlight. Katie adjusted her ball cap. "Ahh!" She winced and pulled her hand away. Tiny shards of glass were embedded in her palms from when she fell.

"Let me see." Eric took her hand in his and looked over the area. "We're going to need to get that taken care of. Got any first aid kit stuff at your parents' place?"

"Yeah. We were always clumsy growing up. Mom made sure to keep stuff on hand." For the first time, Katie wondered if her own mother was ok. She's out of town. She'll be fine. Think about Kacey. "We need to get moving." She pulled her hand away from his.

"You said Oak Hill Avenue, right?"

"Yeah. It's just a few streets over, now." Katie repositioned her bag again and started walking in the direction of her childhood home. This neighborhood hadn't been as ransacked as the rest of town. It was almost eerie how untouched everything looked. Cars lined the streets. It looked like at any moment someone would walk out of their house and check the mail or get in their car to go pick up their kids from soccer practice. Eric kept scanning the area. Wind chimes rattled in the breeze. The notes sang out over the deserted streets. Katie walked closer to Eric. He looked at her and smirked.

"What's that?" Katie leaned her head to the right to get a better look at the vehicles that were parked along the street. At the end of the row, there was a group of people with ripped clothing shoving one another. They were tugging on the door handles of a white car. Some of them were beating their palms against the windows leaving bloody handprints behind. Between the rows of shoulders, Katie saw something move inside the car. "There's someone in there." Her eyes grew wide.

Eric looked at the crowd milling around, "There have to be at least ten of them."

"Right. You coming?" Katie tightened her grip on the knife he had loaned her.

"You're insane." Eric looked at her with disbelief and slight admiration. "You got any combat training?"

"I took karate when I was like eight, and my dad taught my sister and me how to shoot when we were growing up."

"So not really. Ok, look, you know those zombie movies where people always say to go for the head? Well, this time, they seem to be right. The brain is affected. If you take out the brain, you take out the threat. Make sense?"

"Zombies. You know, I always thought that if this ever happened in real life I would be better prepared. I'd just grab my zombie survival kit and hole up at Sam's Club. But now here I am, staring at a horde of zombies, about to run in like a crazy person with a knife." Katie turned her head to look at him, "I'm the person I yell at in horror movies."

Eric chuckled, "Or we could go with option B. Your dad taught you how to shoot? You remember well enough?" Katie nodded while he spoke. "You take the gun and cover me. I'll take the knife. All you have to do is not shoot me. Think you can do that?"

"Yeah." The gun felt awkward in her grasp as he took the knife and handed her the rifle.

"You got this. It'll be a piece of cake." He smiled lopsidedly and winked at her. Once his back was to her his bravery melted away. It was all he could do to make his legs move toward the crowd.

As Eric got closer, he could see a small girl in the back seat of the white car. She was frantically trying to stay as far away from all of the windows and doors as she could. Seeing the girl made Eric tap into his last reserves of courage. He took a deep breath and breathed out slowly. He squared his shoulders and readied his knife. He ran to the closest zombie and rammed his knife into the guy's temple. The blade sunk in up to the hilt. He jerked the knife out and drove it into the eye socket of the next one. Behind him, Katie fired the rifle. Her first bullet ricocheted off of the car's left fender. She cussed under her breath and adjusted her aim. Shoot on the exhale. She could hear her father's voice in her head. She fired another round into the shoulder of one of the zombies that were now focused on Eric. Just a little higher. Her third shot went completely through its head. The bullet had enough momentum that it traveled into the skull of the zombie behind the one she had been aiming at. Both of them immediately dropped to the ground. Katie kept firing, and two more zombies fell to the pavement. Eric stabbed and twisted the knife through the back of a woman's head. He placed his foot on the small of her back and kicked her away from him, freeing his weapon. The force of her impact knocked down another zombie. Eric lifted the knife, clutched it in both hands, and plunged it down into the fallen zombie's skull. His lunge brought him down to one knee.

There were only two left. One charged at Eric and tackled him. Eric lost his grip on the hilt of the knife and rolled onto his back, trying to keep the zombie at arm's length. Katie aimed and pulled the trigger. The gun responded with a light clicking sound. She was out of ammo. While Eric was struggling with one of the zombies, the other one was headed towards her. Blood was smeared across its cheek. It looked at her hungrily and smiled gruesomely as it approached. Katie grabbed the gun by the barrel. The metal seared her skin and the heat made her palms itch. She could see Eric fighting to keep a good handle on the zombie that was on top of him as it writhed in his grasp. Spit drooled out of the zombie's mouth and strung down towards Eric's face. As the second one got closer to her, Katie ran forward to meet it and swung the butt of the gun like a bat into its head. The zombie stumbled. Katie kicked him in the gut knocking him to the ground. She placed her foot on his chest and drove the butt of the gun into his skull with all of her strength until bits of brain matter splattered onto the hem of her pants and across the asphalt.

Katie looked up to see the zombie on top of Eric chomping at the air. His teeth were barely missing Eric's cheek. Katie raced over to them and slammed the butt of the gun into the side of the zombie's head. Eric pushed him off and grabbed the knife that was sticking out of the female zombie's skull. He stabbed the last zombie six times before he allowed himself to begin to breathe again. He looked up at Katie who was standing over him. She was shaking.

Eric stood up slowly and wrapped one arm around her. He pulled her into his chest and she let relief wash over her. Out of the corner of her eye she, saw the little girl move in the car. Katie pulled away from Eric and walked over to the blood smeared vehicle. The little girl looked uncertain.

"It's ok. You can come out now." Katie reassured her.

The girl unlocked the door and pushed it open. She stepped out of the car and looked at all of the dead bodies around her.

"Where are you, parents?" Katie squatted down to look the little girl in the eye. The girl looked towards the bushes on the other side of the car. Katie could see an arm sprawled on the lawn. She took the little girl's hand, "You're going to come with us, ok? We'll keep you safe." The little girl nodded.

"What's your name?" Eric asked.

The girl ducked behind Katie. "Gracie," she said timidly. She held onto Katie's pinkie and ring finger.

"I'm Katie, and this is Eric." Katie stood up, "Let's go this way, ok?" The girl nodded as Katie led her away from the massacre. Katie slung the gun over her shoulder as they walked. They heard the rhythmic whirling of helicopters in the distance, but they couldn't see them yet.

"That's it." Katie pointed at a light blue house in the distance. There weren't any lights on. Katie had a sickening feeling in the pit of her stomach. As they got closer, they could see blood smeared across the siding. Katie let go of Gracie's hand. She ran up the worn, creaking porch steps and pounded on the door. "Kace?" She yelled for her sister as she pressed her nose to the window pane. "Kacey?"

Something moved in the shadows of the hallway to the living room. Katie's heart caught in her throat. She backed away as the lock clicked. The door eased open and Kacey looked through the gap at her sister. Katie jerked the door open and grabbed her little sister in a bear hug. She kissed the top of her head and squeezed her tighter while she wiped the tears out of her eyes.

"Come on, we need to get inside." Katie held the door while the others walked into the house.

Eric started pushing the couch up against the closed door once they were all inside. Katie put her back against the arm of the sofa and pushed with her feet until it slid into place as a makeshift barricade. Kacey went into the kitchen, and they could hear the screech of wood on the tile as she shoved the dining room table against the back door.

"Have you heard from mom or dad?" Katie asked her sister while Eric peered out of the blinds into the street.

"Mom called earlier. She said there are roadblocks around the city, and they aren't letting anyone in or out. I still haven't heard from dad."

Katie walked over to the hall closet and shuffled around the extra toilet paper and the q-tips until she found the first aid kit.

"Here, let me do that." Eric took the plastic box from her, and they went to the kitchen sink. Kacey and Gracie sat on the living room floor and turned on the news. From the kitchen, Eric and Katie could hear the news anchors telling people to stay in their homes. Eric turned on the faucet and let the water run over the tips of his fingers while the temperature adjusted. Once the water was cold, he took Katie's hands and guided them under the stream. She winced a little as the water ran over the tiny shards of embedded glass and the shredded, seared skin that was already beginning to pucker. The cool water offered some relief. Eric pulled the glass out of her palms with a pair of tweezers and then applied antiseptic. While he was wrapping her hands in bandages, Gracie came into the kitchen.

"My mommy always said kisses will make you heal faster." She swayed back and forth from her heels to the balls of her feet while she talked.

Eric smirked and looked at Katie. He took her hands and gently brought them to his lips. He maintained eye contact with Katie as he kissed each of her hands. "I think your mommy was right," Eric said to Gracie while he smiled at Katie. Katie blushed and smiled back at him.

"Let's go back in the living room," Katie shook her head and rolled her eyes at Eric. She put her bandaged hand on Gracie's shoulder and guided her back into the living area.

The mantle was covered in Marine Corps memorabilia, tiny porcelain frogs that Katie's mom had been collecting for years, and a few family photos. Kacey was still sitting on the tan carpet on the floor. Gracie snuggled up next to Kacey and put her head in the other girl's lap. Kacey absent-mindedly stroked Gracie's hair.

Katie and Eric sat down beside the other two. The station was showing footage from a news helicopter as it flew over the town. From the air, you could see the piles of bodies that lined the streets and some of the zombies milling around aimlessly. The video footage shrank into the right-hand corner of the screen as the news anchor came back on.

"The government has taken swift action to contain the situation. Everyone is to remain indoors until the affected citizens can be taken into custody. The CDC would like us to remind you that this epidemic does seem to be contagious. If you are exposed to any bodily fluids of an infected person, please separate yourself from friends and loved ones until you can be reached by officials." A S.W.A.T. team had entered the field of vision on the live footage while the reporter spoke. They meticulously cleared each building. A few team members entered each of the premises. Sometimes they came out with civilians. Sometimes they came out alone. A military man joined the news anchor. His chest was laden with medals that glinted under the florescent lighting. Katie never heard what he was saying because someone pounded on the front door. The knocking drowned out the broadcast.

"This is Sergeant Haskell. Is anyone in there?" The man's voice boomed with authority.

"Yes," Katie yelled as she scampered towards the door, "there are four of us!"

"Anyone bit?"

"No, Sir."

"Alright, open the door slowly, and everyone keep your arms in the air."

Katie and Eric pushed the couch out of the way. Eric unbolted the door and slowly turned the knob. The door creaked open.

"Gracie, honey, put your hands up like this, ok?" Katie said as she raised her hands.

Some members of the S.W.A.T. team entered the house cautiously and started checking the other rooms. Team members started patting Katie, Eric, Kacey, and Gracie down.

"Any weapons?"

"There's a knife and an empty rifle in the kitchen." Eric jerked his head towards the other room. The sergeant motioned for two of his men to check it out.

The soldiers who had been looking through the rooms came back. "All clear."

"Alright, let's move these civilians to the med tents and keep moving." Haskell walked out of the door followed by most of his men.

"This way." One of the soldiers pointed his rifle towards the part of town that had already been cleared.

The men escorting them formed a ring around the four of them as they made their way to the edge of town. They approached a yellow hazmat tent. The soldiers watched them enter the tent and then headed back out to rejoin their team.

"Strip, please." A lady covered in a hazmat suit pulled a thin curtain closed between Eric and the girls. She examined each of the girls, methodically checking them for any lacerations. "What happened to your hands?" The lady looked suspiciously at Katie and gestured to someone at the mouth of the tent.

"I fell on some glass, and I burnt myself." Katie grimaced as the woman undid her bandages to get a closer look.

"I'd like to keep you for observation," the woman backed away from Katie, "just to make sure you didn't get any infected fluids in your cuts." A guard came around the edge of the curtain. "You two can put on the green scrubs over there." The lady gestured to a pile of clothes. "You," she looked at Katie, "need to put on the orange ones. Officer Clifton will show you to an observation tent."

"How...how long are you going to watch her?" Kacey was pale and panicked as she slid the green top over her head. She tugged her hair out of the collar and jerked the bottom of her shirt into place.

"The symptoms should be visible in a few hours if she's been infected. If she's still fine by then, she can find you outside of the quarantine."

"And if she's not?" Kacey's voice rose. The woman didn't say anything, she just looked away. Officer Clifton grabbed Katie's upper arm and started leading her away. Kacey clutched at the officer as he tried to escort Katie out of the tent.

"A little help in here?" The woman called out. Eric pushed aside the curtain as another officer came in to subdue Kacey.

"Watch over them, ok?" Katie said over her shoulder. Eric nodded. His breath quickened, but he tried to remain calm on the outside. He adjusted the green scrubs they had given him and took the two girls outside of the tent to where the red cross was handing out food and water to the townspeople who had been cleared.

Katie was taken to another tent with clear dividers and stretchers. The orange scrubs made her feel like a prisoner.

"Lie down, please." Officer Clifton gestured to the closest stretcher.

"Katie?" The man on the other side of the plastic sheet craned his neck to see her.

"Dad!" Katie smiled at him while the officer strapped her to the cold, metal stretcher. The tent smelled like antiseptic. Her dad was covered in a sheen of sweat. "Dad?"

"Too late for me, Katiebug." He smiled, but his eyes were full of sadness. "Where's your sister, your mom, are they..."

"They're fine. Mom was out of town when it happened, and Kacey was already cleared to go in the first tent."

"Baby girl, if you make it out of here, I—," his body seized up as he tried to speak, "I need you to tell your mom and sister that I love them, ok?" His neck tensed up. His breathing was labored. "Tell them I should have been there for more little league games," Katie's dad groaned in pain as he struggled to get the words out, "and parent-teacher conferences."

"Dad they know how—"

"Katie let me finish. I don't have long." The blood drained from his face. "Tell them I'm sorry, ok? I need you to be strong for them when this is over." His eyes started to dart back and forth, unable to focus. "They're going to need you." He convulsed at the end of his sentence.

"Dad?" Katie fought against her restraints. Her legs and arms struggled to find any give in the straps that had her pinned to the stretcher.

"I need a sedative in here!" Officer Clifton yelled to a nurse.

"I love you, Katie" Her dad looked at her as he tried to keep himself from shaking.

"Dad? Dad!" Katie yelled as nurses surrounded her. She moved her head trying to see her father. She felt a needle slide into her arm. "I love you!" She shouted as her mind became hazy. Her eyes closed even though she fought to keep them open. The sedative took hold of her, and the world went black.

After a few hours, Katie came back to consciousness. She blinked and squinted as a nurse shined a tiny flashlight in her pupils. "Do you know your name?"

"It's Katie." Katie pulled her head away from the nurse.

"Good news, Katie. You appear to have no symptoms of the infection. I'm going to take off your restraints, ok? Just lie still."

"What happened to my dad?" Katie turned her head to look at the empty stretcher behind the plastic.

"He was contaminated. We gave him an injection to help him along peacefully." The nurse touched Katie's arm. "He didn't suffer."

Katie tried to fight back the tears as the nurse removed her restraints.

"Please change into these." The nurse handed Katie a pair of green scrubs as she sat up.

Katie felt numb as she changed her clothes. An officer came and showed her the way out of the observation tent. Katie followed, not really paying attention. It was close to twilight now.

"Katie!" Kacey ran to her sister and hugged her. Her mother followed closely behind and put her arms around both of her daughters.

Katie pulled away and looked at them. "Dad...dad didn't make it." Hot tears ran down her face as the words came out of her mouth. Her mother sat down on the ground and placed her head in her hands. Kacey knelt down beside her mom and cried on her shoulder. Katie's shoulders started to heave as she fought the sobs that were trying to finally escape. Behind her, she felt a strong chest against her back. Katie turned around and buried her face into Eric's chest as his arms encircled her. This was the safest she had felt all day. She let her grief wash over her in waves. She thought about Mia and her dad and all of the devastation she had witnessed.

"Where's Gracie?" Katie mumbled into Eric's shirt.

"She found her aunt. She's with her family now." Eric held Katie tighter as she nodded.

"Here, take one and pass it on." A lady handed them a box of candles with a lighter.

Eric and Katie each took a candle. Katie handed the box to her mom. The survivors all stood in silence, mourning their loved ones. Bodies of the infected were being burned in the streets of the town. They could smell the smoke from outside of the quarantine. The flames of their candles flickered and shone out in the dark as the flames from the burning bodies roared in a crackling cackle. The living and the dead were joined, for one last time, in a vigil of flame.

END

ZOMBIE GAMES

Large bursts of red splattered the wall in a nonsensical design as a whole. Upon closer inspection and in dissecting the design, moving along splat by splat, it became easy to see the clear impressions of heads having been held up and shot at against the concrete wall. The significance for some of the cockier players in doing so lay in the wall's intended purpose. It was not a place for target practice, nor just another guiding wall in the maze; but, in fact, a containment wall for the main game stock of the reserve. Each shot taken at the wall produced a spine-tingling groan from the horde amassing on the opposite side. The sound seeped into the ground below their feet and leached back to the surface underneath the massive barrier so each member of the present hunting party felt the bass of their moans tingle through the soles of their boots. For some, it was akin to receiving a shot of adrenaline at the base of their skull. Others tiptoed past the wall, regardless of their confidence in its structural design.

Not as prominent in the mess of blood and dried brain matter were the resulting chips in the wall from each shot into the concrete. Despite its thickness, the widespread shots from high caliber rifles produced numerous spider webs of cracks. They connected and grew with each additional victory shot. The cracks did not linger along the surface as decoration, though. As the wall fractured outwards, it also fractured inwards with long cracks spanning the width of the wall and appearing on the game's side. The prey were not able to interpret the significance of these cracks, but the damage was significant all the same. While each mark in the wall might have been made in displays of grandeur and bravado on behalf of the hunters, in the end it resulted in a blooming weakness with severe consequences.

These bountiful flaws presented a problem other than the containment of game. When the complex was first built, every spare bag of concrete went into the construction of the containment wall.

A small amount was set aside and used to reinforce several other key structural walls within the maze. After molding these walls, there was nothing left. None of the building materials were conserved with future repairs in mind. The technicians, architects, and all other consultants agreed to sign off on the blueprint and subsequent structure. Management of the facility assured them that the walls were built to last and no thought had been put into rationing materials because "it simply was not necessary." Somehow, the building plans passed and construction moved along at a backbreaking pace. Worker deaths were common and commonly covered up as outside stress related heart attacks. The foundation had been shaky from the beginning, with attempts to steady it with dead bodies and crossed fingers. Even having been constructed at a questionable speed, the resulting maze was deemed up to code the day after the last worker went home – exhausted and under a gag order, like the rest.

Management did not look ahead to the formation of traditions. They did not anticipate their containment wall doubling as a shooting gallery for assholes with the need to boast to their friends. As it happened, those who coded the maze and signed off on its opening did not anticipate Management's lack of interest in discouraging their players from continuing the damaging tradition. With gag orders issued to all involved, dealing with the issue was left up to Management's discretion. Management turned out to be so discreet that no one ever detected any work being done on the retaining wall to maintain its retention and the tradition remained, thriving. Like the ruins of Disneyland in their former glory days, everyone assumed any and all hiccups had been anticipated or were being taken care of behind the scenes in their early stages. Those sorts of procedures forever out of sight of the valued customers. Management enjoyed this traditional consumerism oblivious state of certainty of care for quite a while before someone thought to ask about the crack turned crevice growing along the width of the wall.

Even though someone was curious enough to inquire about the wall's state, it was not directly to Management. A woman in her mid-thirties muttered to a friend on the course as they passed the wall, "I'm not sure that's entirely sound..." Her friend nodded and they both walked on as though it bore no repeating or revisiting. A single utterance turned into another and snowballed until a select group of overcompensating assholes were the only sort to still perform headshots against the crumbling structure. The rest of the visiting public marched or snuck by and shook their head at the falling chips of the wall. Management found themselves forced by public pressure to address the issue – there remained a lone problem: a complete lack of supplies and few creative ideas for substitutes. A paste made with a flour base and industrial glue was the closest any Executive in Management came to a suggestion for the solution of a rather pressing issue. However, a small trial of the stuff proved that the flour-to-glue ratio would leave nothing to prepare food with in the maze's residing region. So, noting how effective the smeared blood and brain matter of the executed game were in concealing the continuously forming cracks, Management tabled the issue of fixing the wall. They paid a mouthpiece to assure the public of the issue's thorough investigation and conclusive results of the containment wall's safety. Then, they silenced the same mouthpiece with a gag order. Since there was no agency above Management in the region to oversee and inspect the maze without prejudice, the matter remained closed; much like the mouths of everyone who knew otherwise.

The day of reckoning came when Management discovered a cover up was not enough to contain the real consequences of passing over the wall's repair. Having provided plausible deniability to all those involved with the wall outside of themselves, Management took the full brunt of the devastating ramifications. The day the dam burst was the downfall of Management's reign over the region. It also led to the uprising of a new breed of esteemed warrior created amidst the resulting chaos.

By chance of time and placement within the maze, a hunting party of seven – cut down to six in the end – rose to the occasion out of necessity with impressive survival instincts and the best possible outcome.

The entrance to the maze was ostentatious. It stood as obvious evidence to anyone passing through of Management's mismanagement of resources. Vast quantities of concrete used to make sculptured doors and overlooking archway could have been conserved to be put towards the most important wall in the entire structure instead. The doors split down the middle so they swung open with dramatic flair, like the entrance to a crypt.

One door displayed a massive ten-foot tall infected with incredible detail etched into its features. It appeared 3D, as though it was lunging out at those approaching its side of the doorway. The crew responsible for the art took the task of adding realism in the design to heart. Arms with greedy hands poised to grab at whatever was within reach jutted two feet out from the main plank of the door. Even the nails on the hands of the infected figure appeared weathered and dirty from feeding.

On the matching panel, a game hunter stood poised with a shotgun pointing outward. His face had been painstakingly carved to display the true grit and cold determination it took to win. The barrel of the shotgun projected about three feet out from the mural to allow for proper proportions and perspective. His finger lay poised on the trigger, prepared for the kill. A cigarette jutted from the corner of his mouth, with fine and intricate detailing giving life to carved smoke. Cigarettes, like many things, had become a luxury akin to coffee or chocolate in the region. Prices dropped as famers re-cultivated their lands and tobacco production increased. For now, a pack cost more than the average citizen's weekly paycheck covered. With a simple cigarette, the man on the door elevated himself to elite status in a financial sense. He presented the ideal image of a man in this new age. It boiled down to being successful and tough with a full body coating of tenacity.

The above archway covering man and beast was simple in comparison. A plain archway was decorated by separate, mounted concrete lettering proclaiming: "*GAME START.*" They were capitalized block letters painted blood red and played the perfect stark contrast to the more elaborate artwork of the doors below.

Teams entered the maze on a timed system behind other hunting parties. Depending on the size of the group and the experience of the party members, the next team sometimes spent the better part of a day waiting for their turn at bat or faced open doors after only ten minutes passed. Currently standing in the corral for pending admittance of hunters was a seven person team. Three women and four men milled about in the open area sharing their anxieties and excitement regarding the upcoming hunt. Chatter died to a minimum to be replaced by last minute stretching as the five minute warning bell sounded.

While each lunged or stretched their arms overhead, they formed a loose circle to listen to the chosen team captain for this hunt. That man was Charlie Weston. At the age of twenty seven he held several maze hunts worth of experience under his belt. Charlie often sat on the receiving end of jokes pertaining to his appearance and how similar it was to that of the entrance's hunter carved into the door. The main difference being Charlie did not smoke and furthermore, could not afford to pick up the habit. Like his other group treks into the maze, he financed this one through a pooling of money. As usual, he divide cost between himself and his assembled peers from the local Training Centre for Maintenance of Battlefield Skills – known as the Centre in common terms. Altogether, it took them two and a half months of frugal saving before enough credits rattled around in the collection jar.

All of the team members trained together at one point or another at the Centre. Their individual skill levels varied, but they worked well together on smaller obstacle courses and during simulations. At the head of the pack stood Charlie, and in descending order of experience ranked Michelle Withers, her twin sister Leslie Withers, Lee Farmers, Leanne Courtney, Andrew Spurner, and Rob Enters. Rob was the youngest of the bunch as well as the least experienced. When Rob confessed to Charlie his desire to attend a formal hunt in the maze, Charlie swung an arm around him and grinned while whispering, "Kid, we're gonna get your cherry popped; just as soon as we can afford it." The collection for their current expedition opened the next day.

In truth, Rob's virgin hunter status provided Charlie with a convenient excuse to open a fund sooner rather than later. It was much easier to rally a team together when the mission started with good reason. Charlie entered the gym with the primary funds jar held out like an idol in his hands. Using a large jar with a slot for credits in the top, Charlie spent a ludicrous amount of time on the graphic pasted to the front of the jar. He drew an old school pinup model from the era before the Infection and the following Eradication. Except, he drew her as an infected; leaving her far more attractive and human in appearance than they were in person. In practiced script, he wrote across the top: "*FOR A GOOD TIME, CALL TIFFANY!*" and across the bottom he wrote the phone number of the Centre. Charlie wore his pride like an ill-concealed hickey. He tried to play it cool, but in the end was far too excited about the trip and his own cleverness to avoid grinning like a fool and showing off his prized jar. Rob blushed and did a poor job of hiding it. The first teasing remark from Leslie prompted him to move with a new urgency to start his individual workout before group training. He turned his face away from his friends as he jogged towards the pull-up bars. When Charlie ribbed him with a final remark of, 'You're welcome!' as he left, Rob tossed a hand up behind him and muttered loud enough for Charlie to hear, "Fuckin' hilarious, Charlie..."

Now the closed gates with the sculpted infected and hunter pair on them stared each team member in the face, save Charlie, who still stood with his back to them. He cleared his throat before launching into a pre-hunt pep talk. This consisted of a couple of reminders about formation as well as the counting and conserving of ammo, then devolved into an all inclusive joke-off at Rob's expense. At the sound of the minute bell, the entire team straightened up and an electric current of nervousness and excitement replaced the recent mirth. Charlie directed a stern gaze towards Rob and spoke in a voice to match, "Are you ready, kid?"

Rob met Charlie's dark eyes with trepidation in response to his suddenly serious tone. He blinked a few times before glancing around at his friends to see if their faces matched Charlie's sudden shift in demeanor. They did not try to hide their enjoyment of Rob's momentary gullibility. He sighed before matching Charlie's tone with sarcastic gravity, "Never been more ready in my life, Sergeant."

It was the sort of response Charlie hoped for. Knowing Rob felt relaxed to the point of being able to joke about the upcoming hunt gave Charlie some assurance of his preparedness for what lay ahead. Charlie's smile grew until it tickled the corners of his eyes with sprouting crows feet. He clapped a hand on Rob's shoulder. "Fuck yeah, you are." Then, he turned back towards the rest of his friends with the same sincere grin and declared, "Let's fuckin' hunt, people!" He hoisted his main weapon, a Remington tactical shotgun, high above his head and let out an overzealous warrior cry. His team followed suit, mimicking his behavior while giggles and sporadic laughter broke up the otherwise serious atmosphere.

As the final ten seconds before their entrance into the maze sounded out in the form of a blaring siren, they assembled themselves in a loose diamond shape. Charlie captained the helm with Rob just behind and to the right of him. This position was reserved for any newcomer to the hunting party. It allowed Charlie to captain the team while everyone else assumed some responsibility for keeping an eye on Rob.

The twins followed – always paired together because out of everyone, they spent the most time on team style fighting. Sometimes while in the maze they split off as a splinter group and followed known dead ends just to clean up the remaining infected. The two held their own with impressive combative techniques against as many as seven infected in a confined space. As the women stepped into their predetermined positions, Michelle turned to her sister and extended a hand toward her and whispered, "Strong apart..."

Leslie clasped her sister's forearm as her sister clasped Leslie's and replied, "...stronger together." From their youngest shared memories in the training ring at the Centre, Leslie and Michelle recalled performing their handshake and accompanying affirmation before starting a session. It qualified as tradition by this point, and they never entered the maze before following through on it. Locked together in a solemn embrace, the two young women were pillars for the concept of strength in numbers. The similarity in their appearance added to this presentation. Both maintained muscular forms and superior knife skills; though, they also scored well on the firing range. Each sister flaunted a head of blonde hair. Michelle wore hers in a mid-length French braid. A salvaged image of *Lara Croft: Tomb Raider* of Pre-I times inspired her at a young age. Leslie kept her hair cut short and pulled back into a tiny ponytail with her side bangs clipped to the side.

Behind the twins stood Andrew and Leanne; Andrew following Michelle and Leanne following Leslie. Their roles were more general than those who preceded them. Neither possessed specialty training, but both were deft in the use of handguns and often attended the shooting range together.

Lee brought up the rear as the team's sweeper. His role consisted of managing long range targets lagging behind the main horde as well as cleaning up the maimed of the infected. Sometimes they stumbled forward leaking putrid fluids from the remainder of a lost arm. Other times lost legs forced them to crawl toward their targets with a mindless continuance. In either condition, Lee took them out with finality.

At last, the deafening sirens stopped their wailing and the tall doors before them opened to permit Charlie's team entrance to the maze. *GAME START.* The doors carried a burst of foul air with them as they swung open to admit the next team. Each member of Charlie's team expected this burst of stench and knew to hold their breaths; all except for Rob. He inhaled as the great tomb opened and then spent the next fifteen seconds of their official run time gagging while hurling half formed insults at his teammates. Charlie did not like to enter the maze with the intention of beating his previous times, but rather aimed for the highest kill count of the day. Rob's planned interruption of their departure made him laugh as hard as the rest of his team.

As soon as the coughing ceased, Charlie took stock of his team once more before facing front and moving forward into the maze with Rob close on his flank. Row by row, their diamond travelled under the archway until the entire team stood trapped in a manufactured warzone and the concrete doors slammed shut behind them.

The terrain within the maze consisted for the most part of desert with lots of obstacles created using large boulders. These rocks were intended for protection and on-field strategy meetings. Not long after opening, though, the more creative hunters with respectable climbing capabilities took to using them for air assaults. Such an attack remained a specialty of the Withers twins throughout their hunts. They hustled up rocks with quick hands, agile steps, and the support of each other. With Michelle standing at the base of a structure, Leslie ran with high and light steps until she jumped and used Michelle's hand as a further boost to the top of the rock. Leslie latched on to the boulder as high up the side as she was able to before hoisting herself the rest of the way up. She then lay down facing the direction she had come from and extended her right hand down to her twin. Michelle, gripping her sister's forearm, scurried up the side while Leslie did her part to haul her up as well. Within seconds, the two stood proud and tall at the highest point available and set up to take potshots at the infected who stumbled by. This routine provided the twins with recovery time after an intense bout of hand to knife combat.

For the moment, they remained in their place in the diamond. It was common for newbies to get too excited when they saw ranking members of a team move out of position. Panic set in when a plan did not unfold as envisioned or expected. After advancing further into the maze and taking part in a few solid kills, Charlie would allow for the more experienced members to loosen up formation. First a confidence builder for Rob, and then fun for everybody. So they advanced in perfect form with Charlie's calm and controlled voice guiding Rob through the first time experience.

In total, Charlie ordered forty five infected for their run with an additional twenty in the dead end zones for the twins to practice on. The number ranked on the low side of Charlie's preferred hunter to infected game ratio, but he knew the adrenaline rush of the maze to be overwhelming without genuine fear in addition to it. He turned to ensure Rob still flanked him and flashed a grin for reassurance when their eyes met. Then, he motioned for them to continue. Seven paces later, the potent smell of their incoming prey puffed out in a fog of decayed air. Around the next left turn, their hunt would begin.

Charlie wanted Rob to take the first kill, so he hauled the young man closer to his side in order to talk him through the next few minutes of his life. In keeping with his cheeky nature, Charlie whispered something to Rob in addition to the vital instructions,

"Since you're paying for it there's no kissing, all right?" Rob's blush spurred Charlie's grin into a quiet snort of laughter. "And here we go…"

Charlie held up a fist in order to bring the rest of the diamond to a halt. He then reached back to yank on Rob's shirt and bring him even closer to the front. Before he could do so, Rob ducked out of the way of Charlie's wandering, midair hand and stepped in line with him. Charlie stayed with the resting diamond of his remaining five team in order to allow Rob the full glory of first kill.

Rob's vision narrowed so he almost forgot about the support of the six people behind him when the first of the infected shuffled into view. The first of sixty five. He raised the gun Charlie had given him a month or so in advance of the hunt to practice with. It was a replica of Charlie's – a Remington tactical shotgun one model older than Charlie's current one. By this point, it felt natural to grip the gun and bring it level in a second. For the first time he saw one of the infected in the flesh and shambling toward him.

The infected game kept in reserve for the maze were not an accurate depiction of what they looked like in the wild – not that any wild infected remained. This new breed of maintained infected were fed just enough to keep them in working condition, but less than they needed to keep them eager for human company during game time. As such, they maintained enough of their muscular structure and outside tissue to function. Their skin continued to decay so their predominant skin color was mottled grey and green. Some tended toward yellow coloring while the absolute freshest of the bunch were a little more purple. They all amassed with the same yellowed eyes, yellowed teeth, and widespread hair loss. Management included infected with missing limbs or ones that were otherwise impaired at a discount. Charlie always paid full price for prime game, so Rob would not encounter any nonpersons leaking decomposition fluids during his first run. For a degree of authenticity, Management left the infected in their original clothing or lack thereof. Some of the infected maintained recognizable attire, while others bore down on participants bare. Between the two categories, it was much more unsettling to turn about-face and find a naked nonperson than a clothed one. More often than not, hunting parties made requests for Management to exclude nude infected from their game. Management denied this request each time. In their opinion, selective gaming was not a valuable use of time, manpower, or other maze oriented resources.

Rob's first date was with a male nonperson of average height who, to his relief, wore a threadbare button-up shirt and torn khakis. Bluish skin draped over fragile bones like an ill fitting bodysuit. Rolls of loose flesh shook with each shaky step as the infected moved toward Rob. Rob's gun remained raised from earlier; he now adjusted his aim to better align with the infected's head. Charlie thought someone's first headshot to be a bloody equivalent of popping the cork on a bottle of champagne after a promotion. In response to his ceaseless reminder, Rob promised to aim high. His finger moved from its position beside the trigger to crook around the small lever itself. He inhaled and as he exhaled he applied the lightest amount of pressure needed to the trigger and felt the slight kickback of the shotgun as it fired. The bullet connected in the small space between the bottom of the nose and the top lip before exploding out the back of its head. Blood splattered over the other infected following the first. It coated them in a thick, black substance that resembled tar rather than blood. This did nothing to impeded their slow, but determined movement forward.

Charlie broke Rob from the spell of his first kill with a proud and congratulatory pat on the back. "Fuckin' A!" Charlie whooped as he tugged Rob back into formation with a gentle insistence. Now that Charlie had had rid Rob of his V-card, it came time to think about the team and their following assault. Taking control, Charlie's tossed commands in the form of encouragement and praise. "All right people, let's fuckin' do this!" By which he meant for everyone to follow the plan of attack as reviewed the night before. Charlie possessed a unique style of command.

Rob cocked his shotgun and waited for the opportunity to take another nonperson down. He already felt addicted to the game and the thrill of the hunt. Now, he would see the same fire come from within Charlie; who had been an addict far longer than Rob. Charlie's voice was heard over the light earplugs everyone wore as well as the increasing moans of the infected wandering closer. He shouted, "All right, people! Advance!" Hurried steps answered Charlie's command as the diamond of hunters moved on quick and quiet feet. The flooring beneath of dry, packed down dirt whipped up dust and debris whenever someone let their foot drag. As they all moved straight ahead down the first path presented to them, Charlie and Rob took charge of clearing the way ahead. They each fired off enough shots to take down the immediate threat. Any infected concealed behind corners and down other possible paths were left to those on the outside of the diamond. Andrew covered the left while Leanne covered the right. The hunters all let off shots with hours of practiced skill behind the trigger. Lee's role did not come into play until the team advanced deeper into the maze and encountered nonpersons in greater numbers and more frequent waves.

After nine infected lay dead wake, Michelle stepped closer to Charlie and tapped him on the shoulder. He turned, saw her gesture to her sister, and understood immediately. She wanted to go play tag team with her twin. In truth, rookie hunts were always a little slower and a little less entertaining for the most experienced players. Michelle and Leslie played on a different level. If able, they would attend hunts solo-ensemble instead of playing as part of a bigger team. With their high level of unique skills, if Management were to change the hunter on the opening door, the Withers twins might be the new 3D feature. Charlie gave a curt nod and the twins bolted. Rob watched the blur of Leslie run by. He then caught sight of the two twins for a brief moment before they darted around a corner. The sound of their blades leaving the sheaves rang out in a clear bell over the constant drone of moaning. Then the far wetter sounds of precise cuts into sagging flesh overtook the air. When those remaining in the diamond passed the corridor down which the two women disappeared, Rob turned to salute goodbye. In doing so, he saw a pile of maimed corpses surrounded by viscous fluids mixing together into a muddy, reddish brown like the leftover paints in an art class. The twins themselves were gone. Having made quick work of the four infected around the immediate corner, they disappeared to find further amusement elsewhere. Charlie's voice disturbed Rob's silent awe of their work, "You'll have to move quicker than that if you ever want to catch those two in the act."

Charlie remembered his first hunt with the twins. Even though he captained their hunts, the twins were more experienced and better fighters. Their inability to include other people on the same playing field as each other knocked them down to second in command. The first time he hunted with them was his second hunt in total. At the end of the day, any stragglers in the waiting area with inclinations toward the maze, but lacking in party members gathered together to form a team. Charlie knew the twins from brief encounters pre or post training at the Centre, but nothing more than pleasantries or compliments on combat technique. Along with nine other people, the twins and Charlie entered the maze that night without knowing each other and exited planning for future hunts together. He both admired and envied them for their bond and the way that bond translated into their performance in the maze.

The diamond advanced quicker now, knowing the chances of encountering infected before reaching the opening checkpoint decreased every moment the twins were on the loose. The opening checkpoint was a circular area in the center of the maze with five different paths sprouting in all different directions. It was not difficult to find one's way out of the maze, but some paths were a much more direct route to the exit than others. Charlie knew the end result of each road and he planned to take them down the most nerve-wracking of the bunch. A small smile leaked onto his face in spite of his desire to surprise Rob by leading them past the glorified and feared containment wall.

Between their current station and the checkpoint, Rob downed another three infected. Charlie backed off a couple of obvious shots just so Rob could have another go. The kid grinned with pride each time a nonperson hit the ground and spilled their foul innards. Charlie felt his own spark of pride in Rob and the progress on display. He turned in quick checks on the rest of his team while they moved and noticed a general nod of approval going around in regard to Rob's abilities. It pleased Charlie that his fondness for the kid spread to his other training buddies. He thought Rob made a good addition when they had been without a new face for a almost a year.

The hollow pops of Lee's hunting rifle as he undertook cleanup duty sounded out in intermittent bursts. As of yet, he remained calm in the background of the killing; waiting to be needed. Leanne and Andrew were barely out of the shadows in comparison. Each took more shots thus far than Lee, but also held back in order to focus more so on judging Rob and his capabilities. This first stretch of road leading into the central workings of the maze served as an excellent combination of ice breaker and nerve wrangler for first timers and newly formed teams. People appreciated the opportunity to hone their confidence alongside their camaraderie. It worked well for Charlie's team, as they were all walking in sync by the time they reached the circular gap surrounded by the multiple roads. Here, they paused to catch their collective breath and check on ammo.

"So kids, how is everyone doing? Rob? Still good?" Charlie leaned in with one hand on Rob's shoulder to ground him.

The young man gasped a little in response before forming words. His voice tingled with lingering excitement, "Charlie, this is fuckin' incredible."

Charlie beamed at this. "Atta boy! The lad's even starting to sound like the greats." He winked at his other teammates who long since grew used to Charlie's perpetual swearing. Some adopted his speech while others shocked themselves when expletives snuck into their otherwise benign sentences. The twins brought their own foul mouths with them to the gym, but Charlie provided consistent support of their habit with his own creative wording.

Staying in formation during weapons check at a cleared checkpoint was not a requirement. During this less strict formatting, Leanne and Andrew drifted closer together. They denied any questions about dating, but did not hide their affection for one another. The two did not go so far as to make out in the middle of a hunt, but Andrew tucked Leanne's loose hair behind her ear and openly let his hand linger on her cheek. She smiled in return and leaned into the rough palm against her face. Everyone else averted their eyes without the requirement of a verbal request before doing so. Andrew spoke low to Leanne, "You good?" As simple a question as it was, Andrew put all his care for her behind it. He ran his thumb along her cheekbone with a tenderness reserved for Leanne. She smiled and provided an equally simple response in the form of a nod. Her hand came up and lithe fingers curled around Andrew's much larger hand. They stayed silent while staring at each other.

Even Charlie let them have a moment of peace before clearing his throat with great vigor to break the fragile spell over them. "All right, kids, let's move out. We're heading down the northeast path."

Rob did not notice the looks of anticipation passed between the four more experienced hunters. They knew what lay at the end of the northeast path. Every one of them was eager to see Rob's reaction. The first time of a virgin hunter passing the containment wall was always memorable. Though many newbies knew of the containment wall before entering their first game, there was no way to prepare for an encounter with the real thing. The diamond advanced toward the landmark wall of the maze with four of the five watching for the fifth's reaction. Another mile of terrain with the addition of rock blockades and obstacles lay between them and the wall. Their forward momentum continued like a steady pulse. Each step over a boulder and each infected downed brought them closer to their mid-game goal.

In the distance, a loud elephant gun went off. Rob started at the noise; but the thunder of the shot seemed to turn Charlie bitter. He muttered, "Fuckin' assholes and their big fuckin' guns... Hard not to hit something with a cannon slung over your back..." The man had little patience for the weaponry flamboyance or testosterone fueled competitions practiced by other teams. Charlie admired a hunter for their skill, not their machinery. He knew the blaring blasts so close by meant someone was compensating for their lacking manhood with a headshot against the restraining wall. He shook his head at the practice every time the misfortune of witnessing it fell upon him. No one in Charlie's teams practiced the tradition as a condition of joining him for a group hunt. He understood the implications of each bullet's impact on the increasingly fragile wall. One day, one too many victories celebrated, one fewer wall, and a lot fewer people.

The Weston team stalled when Charlie drew them to an abrupt halt with a fist held in the air next to his head. They remained stationary out in the open of the path. Lee popped a round into the head of a nonperson at his feet. The entry point of Andrew's shot showed up black against pale skin; dead through the center of the thing's throat. A kill shot for anyone living, but not sufficient to terminate an infected. Turning to look, Andrew greeted Lee with a shrug at the too-low shot. Charlie's hand remained in the air throughout, clenched in a tight fist. He often lowered his hand as soon as the team rooted itself in place. When his hand stayed hovering in the air as it did now, it was a sign of potential danger. Charlie wanted absolute silence in order to assess the situation; a rare request from the noisy and outgoing man. The rest of the team soon realized the danger Charlie sensed when a quiet tremble started beneath their feet.

At first, the ground shivered like a whisper meant to fade. The top layer of dry dirt lifted off the ground and became airborne as a result of the vibrations. Charlie turned inward to address everyone in his command. In a stern voice, he directed them to take cover behind the nearest obstacle and cover their faces with their hands. A great hustle took up among the team as they dispersed to take shelter and await Charlie's next order.

Rob looked about with confusion before Charlie grabbed his shirt collar and reoriented him with the firm grasp. Charlie kept his tone light, but still serious, "Listen, kid, shit's about to hit the fan so I need you to listen to me. You can keep doing that, yeah?" He stared into Rob's eyes, trying to impart the importance of their decisions during the next few minutes.

Rob blinked once before nodding and blurting out, "Tell me what's going on when we're safe?" It turned out to be the most polite way to ask Charlie to explain what the fuck was going on at the most convenient time possible.

Charlie exhaled in relief at Rob's compliance. He nodded once in promise of explanation before jerking Rob's collar and leading him to a barricade large enough for the two men to huddle behind. Charlie released Rob's shirt when they were both crouched against a structure made of large boulders bound in chicken wire. He turned to the young man by his side and huffed out an explanation. "You know the containment wall?" Rob nodded. "You know the target shooting tradition that goes with it?" Rob nodded again. "That wall's been a wreck waiting to happen for years. I think some asshole just wrecked it." Rob did not know how to respond to this revelation, but it was not with a nod.

Meanwhile, the shivering and trembling of the ground evolved into a full blown tremor. The obstacles they hid behind were stable, but smaller rocks jumped across the ground as it shook. Shouts from the same direction as the earlier shot played out alongside the shaking of the ground. Before Charlie shared his worrying thoughts with the rest of the team, a great thunder took up and consumed all the angry voices. After this, the dry clash of concrete breaking from the containment wall and tumbling to the ground below became the leading noise. The wall was falling to pieces less than a quarter mile from their current position. More concrete thunder erupted through the air and continued for a few minutes. There was another deep shudder from the ground below the five separated team members. Charlie did attempt to shout a warning over this cacophony, but the incoming tidal wave of powdered concrete carried atop a foul wind interrupted him. A fog descended over the area before the dust and floating debris settled on the now unmoving ground. The rest of Charlie's team appeared in fuzzy forms, gaining clarity the longer they waited out the dust cloud. Andrew and Leanne knelt behind a single large boulder, tucked into one another for protection. Charlie could not see Lee and assumed him to be crouched behind a barrier behind them somewhere; given his backmost position in the diamond formation. When the surrounding air was, for the most part, dust free, each of the five stood up and stepped from behind their individual choices for shelter. They came together by the rock and chicken wire formation chosen by Charlie and Rob. Though each held their own on the field and prepared for the worst before each hunt, an newfound unease permeated their following conversation.

Before Charlie got out a reassuring word, a second wave comprising entirely of sound and stench swallowed his voice. The spine-tingling groan of the horde lacked the dulling effects provided by the thick concrete wall under normal circumstances. Its sudden intensity raised the hairs on the necks of all those present. With the collective exhale of the freed infected arrived a horrible stink. The smell assaulted the nose of anyone trapped inside the inner workings of the maze. Worse than the initial scent was the enduring decay floating free. Without admitting why, they all spat onto the ground. The taste of death stuck to the back of their throats and coated their tongues.

This time Charlie spoke without further interruption by disaster. He was not military and did not put up a front for his team. Charlie, like the rest of them, was scared shitless. He did not need to explain what had happened up the road from them. Yet, he felt obligated to approach the obvious danger of their newfound situation. He tried clearing his throat a couple of times to get the spit flowing, but it only stirred up the rotting taste in his mouth. The opening line of his reassuring speech turned out to be less motivational than planned when all he mustered was a breathless, "Fuckin' hell..."

The severity of the maze's sudden change in design had yet to set in as they recollected their wits. Charlie snapped out of it before anyone else and, at last, found his commanding tone, "Fuck! We have to go. Now. NOW. Move! Back the way we came from, forget a tight formation, but for fuck's sake, stay together. Let's go!" In keeping with the rest of the hunt, Charlie took it upon himself to lead Rob around by the collar of his shirt. It already rested misshapen against Rob's collar from the constant stress of Charlie's tight grip.

The team reversed their course and retraced their steps back down the initial road leading to the opening checkpoint. By luck of their choice of their preplanned route, it was a straight shot back to the entrance and relative safety. Having cleared their return path, Charlie broke into a fast jog followed the rest of his team. He was far less worried about encountering one or two stray infected on their way back than he was about encountering hundreds on their way forward.

Each member of the team touched down on the solid doors in similar manner of desperation. Given the solid structure of the doors, they did not budge. No one expected the doors to upon first impact, but worry sewed its discord among them when there was no answer upon their continued violent banging and cries for help.

Rob turned to Charlie, his mentor, and asked with a shaking voice, "What the hell are we going to do, Charlie? There are protocols for this sort of thing, right?"

Charlie did not know what to say in order to reassure Rob of their safety, but also impart the severity of their circumstances on the rookie. He shook his head, but tried to keep Rob calm nonetheless, "No, there are no protocols. Management's word of the day is going to be 'unforeseen.' Fuck! Okay, we're going to stay here and wait for an announcement, which *is* going to come any minute now. We're not going to think too far beyond holding down this position and waiting for some explanation. Okay, Rob?" Charlie stared down the young man until he nodded; a degree of uncertainty still plaguing his features. He turned to the remainder of his team and waited for their more controlled responses. One by one, they, too, nodded with a better handle on their emotions.

The announcement came as Charlie predicted, but the message was not as helpful as he hoped it would be. Through speakers imbedded in the walls of the maze, a booming voice with computerized calmness spoke to them, "Attention hunters, the containment wall separating game from the reserve has burst. The entrance and exit doors will be sealed shut until further notice. Management is attempting to control the game overflow. Conserve ammunition and maintain distance from any visible nonpersons during this time. Thank you for your cooperation and patience." The voice cut off.

Despite waiting for another minute and praying for further instruction, nothing came. Genuine panic set in for all present and they turned to Charlie for guidance. Charlie glanced around at all of them, looked behind him, and then turned back to them with a shocked expression dawning over his face. "Listen, you guys, I don't know what the fuck they expect us to do in here, but our best shot is finding Michelle and Leslie. Those two are like fuckin' lemurs on steroids. If anyone can find a way out that Management hasn't close off, it's them, yeah?" A small comfort, but it was all Charlie had to offer them in this moment. The looks of despair did little to comfort him in return. He continued, "Look, you guys, I know this is fucked and I'm sorry, but I'm just as clueless here. The only thing we can do is enter game mode and survive, yeah?" This time, he looked around to find timid nods from the three more experienced players. Rob needed to be looked after, though. Charlie addressed him specifically, "Rob? Rob, I need you to focus and follow me. Listen to me." He tugged on the familiar, deformed collar to bring Rob in closer. "It's still just a game. We're still just on another hunt, but now, we're getting extra game for free. It's a fuckin' bargain, I tell ya! Goddamned dream any other time." He forced it, but managed to grin at the end of that to reinforce a sense of normality. Rob nodded with a measure of conviction this time and shifted his gun in his hands in preparation for moving out. This brought a genuine grin to Charlie's face. "Atta boy. For now, though, we're gonna switch up to handguns." Charlie withdrew his own Remington 1911 from his side holster. He then reached around and withdrew its twin to hand to Rob. "I know you're not as comfortable with this one, but you're still a helluva shot with it. We don't have the luxury of time so shotguns are out. Keep count of your ammo." Charlie handed Rob three fifteen round clips in addition to the one in the gun. "Pocket these." Charlie turned to address his friends now counting on him to lead them through this. "At least you're with the best in the worst situation, right?" He waggled his eyebrows at the end in desperation

Lee snorted at Charlie's attempt to ease tensions, but smiled with authenticity. Andrew nodded, though his arm remained as a protective barrier around Leanne's shoulders. She did not cling to him, but leaned into his embrace. She was the first to speak of the three, "You're fuckin' full of it, Charlie. Lucky for you, the rest of us aren't. Let's do this." She shrugged out from under Andrew's embrace and reloaded her current clip having expended five bullets. Leanne turned back to him with a smile masking her fear, "You good to go, babe?"

She surprised Andrew by addressing him with a pet name, but it revealed her worry that they might not be able to find a way out this time. He understood and followed her lead in reloading his current and checking his gun. "Good to go, hon."

Lee checked his pocket to ensure his clips were easy to reach. He addressed Andrew when he spoke, "Yep, good to go, honey!" This was the tipping point allowing the atmosphere of doom surrounding them to lighten. Even Rob in his state of rookie-tinged panic laughed aloud.

Charlie smiled at the change in his team's tone. "Okay, all right, Leanne's right. Let's fuckin' do this! Diamond formation with a couple of switches; I'll lead, Andrew beside me watching the right, Rob behind me closest to the wall, Leanne beside him and behind Andrew, Lee taking it up the rear where he likes it."

Lee interjected, "You know you're the only one for me, Charlie!"

Charlie smiled before continuing, "We're moving left staying along the perimeter as much as we can. The twins went off that way and knowing them, they're perched on a rock somewhere taunting infected and waiting this shit out. Let's move!" The team reassembled themselves into a tight formation. Rob did not have the option of being led by Charlie or playing standby any longer, but Charlie placed him in the most protected position in the new diamond. He appreciated this thoughtfulness more than he was able to express right now.

The team took off, moving forward with steady determination. Whenever the right wall opened into a new path, Andrew and Leanne both turned with practiced swiftness to address any approaching threat. Charlie made smart choices on the course under normal circumstances and he somehow managed to keep his head in this high stakes game, as well. The perimeter allowed them to keep an entire flank covered and expend far less ammunition than if they wandered deeper into the failing structure. Moving onward, Andrew and Leanne continued to pivot with guns pointed at every possible point of attack. They soon reached the leftmost wall of the maze, at which point, they turned and moved north in hopes of joining back up with the twins. Even though they remained glued to the outside wall of the maze, it was necessary for them to move forward into more dangerous territory. After passing three clear openings into different paths, Andrew and Leanne started letting off an increasing number of rounds each time they pivoted. When their clips dwindled down to one or two bullets, they reloaded and continued with professional cool. Charlie, Rob, and Lee had not yet needed to raised their weapons. Thus far, the attack expanded outwards into the maze from the outermost wall to the right. This funneled all the infected game toward the left and the current location of the Weston team. Andrew and Leanne were getting plenty of use out of their guns because of the horde's direction. When they next paused to let off a combined total of seventeen rounds, Charlie slipped an extra clip into each of their back pockets. Without pause for thanks, they carried on.

A godsend came in the form of the Withers twins perched atop the highest available obstacle in the vicinity. The women did not notice their team approaching, as they were rather involved in a discussion. Neither was quite sure if their new high kill counts would go up on the competitor's board because of the circumstances and they were both concerned by this fact. Approaching, Charlie heard Leslie finishing with, "—I bet they don't even give us a voucher for next game in quiet recognition."

"You're already expecting this place to reopen, Les?" Her and Michelle turned in synchronicity to take in Charlie and the others. They mirrored each other's smiles at his sudden arrival.

"What the hell else are we supposed to do for fun, huh?"

"Seems like you've been doing just fine as is..." Charlie referred to the massive pile of infected corpses surrounding their boulder. A small slope lead up to the twins as their body count excelled and nonpersons climbed over the dead to reach their food source. It added to the horrible smell of the maze, but the mountain of bodies dripping with pus and blackened blood made for a magnificent sight.

Michelle snickered at her twin before dropping down from the rock obstacle while avoiding her trophies to join her team on the ground. She raised a hand flat in the air as Leslie jumped a little further out and down, bracing her own hand against Michelle's level palm to slow her fall so she landed with feline grace. Leslie stood and went on, "We have an idea."

"I guess that 'strong apart, stronger together' mantra shit really works. What's the plan, ladies?" Charlie used a cough to cover the sigh of relief he felt at having found the people more qualified for stealth missions than himself.

Michelle started, "You had to right idea of sticking to the perimeter, now we just have to get you lot a little higher."

Leslie picked up where she left off. "At the back wall, about two thirds of the way in is the highest point in the entire maze. If you can manage the climb, getting over the outside wall shouldn't be a problem for anyone here."

"Sound good?" Michelle knew Charlie remained the leader through technicality, so she followed procedure and confirmed their escape rout with him.

Charlie blinked and tried to envision their planned path in his mind. Adrenaline and the sudden overweight responsibility on his shoulders clouded his mapping skills. He trusted the Withers like nobody else when it came to instincts and follow through, so he nodded. "Let's do it. Everybody here good to move out toward the back wall?" A round of nods, much surer than before. "Okay, it might get a little dicey in there, but hang on. You got me, Rob?"

Rob did not care to be singled out, but he understood Charlie's concern for Rob as well as his impact on the rest of the team. He was a rookie in a tense game of cat and mouse; and he was still unsure about who or what between his peers and the infected was which. He nodded like the others, hoping to gain some of their confidence by faking his own. "I got it, Charlie. I'll stick close and follow your lead."

Charlie's unconsciously tensed shoulders lowered at this level of understanding from a newbie. Their situation was grave and playing it safe was their sole option with the possible outcome of survival. "Great." He turned back to the twins, "Why don't you two take the lead?"

Michelle and Leslie both rolled their eyes at each other before Michelle answered, "Obviously." Leslie smiled at her sister. She and Michelle each reloaded their current clips and checked that their sheathed blades were accessible. Michelle took the lead in the diamond with Leslie half a step behind her to watch her sister's back. "Mind the bodies, they sort of piled up while you were gone." Her words were smug with pride at the two dozen corpses mounded up against each other. A mélange of green, gray, blue, purple, yellow, and black skin tones and innards spilled onto the ground around the boulder as though they worshipped at the Withers' alter. Careful steps around the mess drove them closer to their destination. Now that the twins were in charge, there was less pressure placed on Andrew and Leanne to cover the right flank. Leslie beat them with consistency at the shooting range, so she was a miracle in the moment. She discarded old clips with a single bullet remaining as they travelled, never firing her gun dry. The clips were replaced with fresh ones in an instant and she continued to take down anything shambling toward her team from inside the maze. Andrew and Leanne breathed easier with Leslie taking charge of coverage.

The overall sense of improvement of their predicament declined as soon as nonpersons dribbled out from the right hand paths to block their current route. Michelle at last had an excuse to raise her gun while she downed the infected blocking their way forward. She fired using the focus of intense aggression toward the reserve game. The twins never got scared, they got angry. Furrowed brows adorned serious faces as they led.

Headshots made each infected go down in a celebratory burst of black and red as a bullet mangled their faces before lodging in their rotting brains. The closer to the back wall they got, the more dismay mounted in the form of human corpses lying among the infected ones. Some were not so lucky as to escape the horde with height or cunning. Several times, the Weston team came upon a dozen nonpersons ripping the intestines from a fresh kill of an inexperienced hunter. The twins took these ones down with their knives. Their faithful Bowie knives fit into their palms like missing pieces as they took to dispatching the amassing crowd. Justice was the slicing of blade through flesh and the sinking of a dagger deep into the dead eyes of an infected before turning and finding the temple of another. The twins engaged in a combative dance; the end result being another pile of leaking corpses at their feet when finished. There was nothing to be done for the hunters beneath the stinking heap. Each time they moved on with a pang of regret, but remained focused on their own escape.

They reached the back wall without a major incident impeding their progress. Michelle snugged herself into the corner to regroup and go over the next part of the plan in more detail. "Okay, everyone whole?" She huffed out the question while she caught her breath. A circle of nods followed. "Good. Part two—"

Leslie interrupted her twin with a shout directed toward Lee. In a momentary lapse, he wandered back to scope out the last human victim they came across about ten feet away and in doing so, also wandered closer to a path opening. Though the team cleared each opening as they came across it, there was no guarantee of them remaining clear. This was obvious as a nonperson reached from around the corner to snag Lee's shoulder before sinking its yellowed teeth into the soft flesh of his neck. Lee screamed and turned to fire his rifle into the thing's head. The length of the barrel of the gun hindered his shot, and the only damage was to the infected's right ear. The nonperson roared at the sound and released Lee's neck, but then bit back down with more force. Thick, red blood spurted from the man's neck while he fell to his knees in pain.

Charlie was the next to scream, but his was a warrior cry. He bolted toward Lee and the nonperson latched onto his neck with his gun raised. Pausing for second, he popped the thing in the head so the force pushed backward and off of Lee. Meanwhile, Lee crumpled to the ground in the opposite direction of the infected, still crying out. Charlie dropped down beside him and rolled him over so Lee's head rested in his lap. "Oh fuck, Lee! Fuck, man! Leanne! Get the kit, get the fuckin' kit!" He whirled around, but no one was moving. Charlie knew it, but would not admit to Lee being a dead man. "Fuck, fuck, fuck…"

Lee coughed blood onto Charlie's pants. It foamed at the sides of his mouth each time he gasped for air. Charlie bent his head and grabbed Lee's hand, squeezing it as tight as he would a trigger. He stared down into his friend's eyes. The man below him knew; he knew it was over and there was nothing to be done to the contrary. He squeezed back Charlie's hand as hard as he could with his life slipping away. Try as he might, the closest he got to a smile was a pained grimace as the last spurt of blood rose and dribbled down Lee's chin from his gaping mouth. The man shook a few times before resigning to his fate. He went slack in Charlie's grasp and his head lolled to the side in confirmation of his end.

Part of the Post-E procedure was a vaccine for those in the developed regions to prevent against further infection of the remaining human populace. It offered a small blessing to the Weston team. Knowing Lee to be vaccinated, no one's conscience was in danger of being burdened with ensuring their friend stayed down.

Charlie climbed to his feet after resting Lee's head on the ground as gently as he knew how. He wiped at his eyes, refusing to cry in front of his team when they needed him to keep his shit together. Michelle was the stoniest of the bunch in tense situations, but it helped her to survive. Charlie looked to her cool demeanor for direction; he felt lost. She understood and rallied the troops. For now, she played the bad guy and insisted they move on without attending to Lee beyond dragging his body behind a barrier for cover from more wandering infected. She snapped at the team now so disheartened and misplaced in their current goal. "Listen. I'm Captain Bitch right now, and we're moving out. Let's go." Leslie followed her sister without question which prompted the rest of the diamond to do so, too. Everyone except for the twins looked back to where Lee lay hidden and bit their lips to keep from sobbing.

The team crept along the back wall of the maze. Leslie, Andrew, and Leanne all walked sideways, crossing their feet to move along with the rest of the formation. The number of infected they came across exiting pathways increased as they moved closer to the source of the game leak in a critical vie for their survival. Clips were reloaded more often and Charlie dolled out replacements like candy on Pre-I Halloween. He tucked them into his teammates pockets as they ran out and alternated between this, taking his own shots, and watching out for Rob. Charlie moved to the back of the diamond to maintain Lee's sweeper position. He walked backward with the diamond as infected appeared to ooze from the walls and shuffle along the restrictive width of the road leading to them. Rob remained the safest of the bunch, taking far fewer shots than anyone else.

Soon, Michelle tagged the shoulder of her sister and pointed forward to their objective. A stack of five boulders bound together with thick ropes and complex knots leaning high against the outer wall. It glowed with the mere prospect of the salvation it offered. Charlie called from the back, "You're covered! Fuckin' go!" Leslie spun and nodded once before she holstered her gun and broke into a run alongside her twin.

They did not abandon the group as Rob thought, but rather went on to station themselves atop the rock as they had done many times before. Michelle redrew her weapon to take out the infected amassing from the other side of the obstacle. After she gained thirty feet of clearance between the horde and the boulders, she holstered the gun once more. Leslie lay on her stomach while Michelle crouched down behind her and grabbed her ankles in preparation to bring up the rest of the team. Michelle maintained a firm grasp as Leslie wormed her way over the side. There, she waited. Michelle hollered to the others, "Get your collective ass moving! Forty feet, lady and gents! Pretend you're on fire and fuckin' go!"

Andrew grabbed Leanne's hand before taking off toward the roped boulders. They hugged the outside wall to stay out of reach of the infected still pouring from every orifice inside the maze. Charlie shoved Rob in their direction, "Fuckin' go, kid. You're covered, too." Rob sprinted after the other four, thinking Charlie was right behind him. It was not until an infected grabbed for him and then seemed to drop dead without reason. A hole in its head directed Rob to look back at Charlie. The team's leader stayed put as the others ran in order to provide them clear passage. Having been told to do so by the man himself, Rob took up in a run again. He watched Leslie haul Leanne up the side of the obstacle before she helped Andrew up the same way. Since he weighed much more, Andrew first used the anchored ropes to pull himself part way up to meet Leslie. Rob followed suit and scrambled up the side toward Leslie's saving grace of a hand.

He felt hands on the bottom of his feet and screamed at the thought of being yanked down into a crowd of nonpersons. As it turned out, Charlie was not as far behind Rob as Rob thought. The man was pushing Rob closer to Leslie as infected pushed in from all directions. Andrew and Leanne resumed Michelle's duty of clearing the encompassing area so Charlie had a safe chance to get on their level. After the soles of Rob's boots left his hands, Charlie, too, scrambled up the rock wall with adrenaline fueled agility. He clasped Leslie's forearm as soon as it came within reach and hoisted himself up before offering her a hand in return. A surprise nonperson snapped at the air Leslie's hands occupied seconds before as she rose.

They were safe for the moment, but no one paused to catch their breath or talk. So long as they stood atop this rock mound, they were still inside the maze. Michelle darted to the wall. Her eyes rested at the same height as the wall, so she reached up and pulled herself onto the ledge with strong arms. On either side of the "*GAME OVER*" exit, a ten foot wide river ran along the back wall. Upon swinging her legs over and staring down into the dark below, Michelle declared, "Doesn't look too far," and jumped. Leslie flashed a smile at her twin's abrupt escape after all the trial that propelled them to this point; but she followed in a similar fashion and leapt over the side without parting words.

The team listened for a corresponding crash onto unseen rocks below or cries of pain if it was too far. A much more comforting sound arrived. Two small splashes spaced close together followed by Leslie's tinkling voice and genuine laughter called to them, "Jump, you fuckin' pussies!"

The remaining team members burst out laughing. Charlie spoke through choked laughter, "No reason why we can't all go over at once, right?" He grabbed Rob's shirt collar one last time within the maze and hauled the man over the edge with him.

They fell over thirty feet before connecting with water made cold by the night's falling temperature. Andrew and Leanne landed about five feet from them. They broke the surface one after another, all gasping for breath and in mild shock from the cold. The Withers twins sat on the opposite bank, soaking wet, but alive and safe. They waved in unison to their friends still bobbing in the river. "Care to join us?" Leslie called out over the sound of a mellow current and dulled cries of the remaining game inside the maze.

They swam and emerged from the bank shivering. Andrew was out first and reached for Leanne before disappearing her into a massive hug. She threw her arms around his midsection with equal passion. Charlie helped Rob out, but met him with a less intimate pat on the back.

Charlie exhaled, "*Fuck...*" All but one member of his team stood safely next to him outside the walls of a concrete nightmare. For now, the emotion was too much to sift through. He recognized Lee was dead, but the overwhelming relief of everyone else being alive overtook all other thoughts.

Rob broke through his peaceful veneer of short lived ignorance. "Will Management ever admit to what they've done?"

Charlie's eyes opened to reveal a significant and heavy sadness in them, though he tried to be uplifting. "Not a chance, kid. But I bet we get in for free anytime if they ever open this place again." He closed his eyes again to contain the tears threatening to spill down his face. Even now, he tried to be a leader – especially for Rob. *'Kid's gonna be scarred for fuckin' life... I'm gonna be scarred for fuckin' life... Oh fuck, what the fuck did I lead us into?'*

The prospect of free hunts was not enough compensation for their loss; not nearly enough.

Game start. Game over. Cover up. Repeat for profits. Certainly, the cycle would continue under new Management.

END.

ZOMBIE DIARIES

Professor Mole paced around the office. These were troubling times. He had never really heard of anything like this, not on a medical level at least. In terms of the tension, devastation and panic it was causing, he had many examples. The camps of Auschwitz, the trenches of World War One, Europe under the ravaging of the Black Death... except this was so much worse. Or was it? As a history professor, he realized he couldn't say that. Yes, this was some strange combination of war and disease, but isn't it the same as what the Japanese went through in Hiroshima and Nagasaki, or what the Native Americans experienced at the hands of the Pioneers? It felt so much worse to be caught in the middle of it, of course. But the horrors he was seeing were no worse. If anything, he was tasting a dose of what it must have been like to be a victim of warfare and disease, to be a peasant in those times.

Except he was quite unlike a peasant. Professor Mole had been an avid survival enthusiast, a humble follower of medical journals and a learned historian. His areas of expertise had been demographics. All of this had elevated him above the peasantry of his times, of the new world order, into a leader of sorts. He had never imagined becoming a leader. He was an introvert, a nerd, not exactly an outcast but not quite admired or desirable either. But the event had changed everything. Of course it had. At first he was still one of the peasants. In a time when sheer physical prowess, gunman-ship and vehicles had been a priority, even a fairly fit man in his late forties couldn't keep up. He had fallen behind a number of leaders, all young and powerful, many with military backgrounds, with guns and trucks. But one after the other they had fallen. They served their purpose well and he didn't resent them or look down on them. They were just not cut out for long term survival, for long term leadership. Meanwhile, he, the inconspicuous middle aged man, had gradually shown his uses to the refugees and they had eventually come to invite him to lead them. And here he was, up in a bell tower, looking down on a college campus not unlike the one where he used to teach, watching his students and followers milling around like busy worker ants.

The place was reinforced, the walls scaled with chicken wire, the wire electrocuted, a moat outside the walls was in progress but would not be complete for a few months yet. The square had been given over to crops but the sundial remained to remind everyone to not lose their ability to keep time or count the days. Some of his students had manufactured biofuel, but it corroded the engines of their trucks so much that even when only one vehicle a day patrolled they needed regular dismantling and cleaning. They had built a fort the likes of which Professor Mole had only seen in news reports and history books. All to keep *them* out. They were not peasants, or refugees, not any more. They were survivors, militants, a tribe. And neither would they, like the peasants of times gone past, go undocumented. Professor Mole was going to make sure of that. He kept his diary and his faithful students typed it, backed it up, copied it by hand and etched it. Anything to ensure that at least one copy survived this fallout, that, should everything fall apart or should they fade out along with their memory, at least one book would tell the world what happened that drove them to this and how they survived.

Professor Mole looked at the sundial in the square, squinting to make it out properly. It was around four. Probably later than that, as it was still quite warm and Summery and the days were very long yet. But nevertheless, as the sundial marked four, he sat down at his desk, pulled out a fresh notebook and began writing.

August 1st, 2019.

Mole Camp, Texas (?).

The students are progressing well. They have uncovered many of their skills by now and everyone knows what they can achieve together. As I mentioned before, but it bears repeating, as everyone brings their skills to the table we find society advances. Those who kept hidden skills out of modesty, shame or shyness are now either openly helping, cast out or dead. Hiding a skill is as bad to the formation of a society as hiding a supply of water, food or a weapon. After making my students understand this they became more open. They also necessarily became hostile towards those who concealed their skills, which isn't useful, but isn't in my power to control. Some have died, but we must live on.

Currently Thomas and the Evans boy are trying to clear our engines out. The use of biofuel was a genius conception, but it is starting to wear our vehicles. We needed Smith, our resident mechanic, to work on them, but she had become uncooperative following Tyler's remark that for our society to survive she must use her womb and not her brain. I hope both of them adopt a more helpful attitude soon, or they will both become outcasts and, when the tribe turns on someone, there is not much I can do. I am shockingly powerless as their leader. It serves me well to know that tribes all too often become a brute-force democracy and it pleases me to know now that, however violent this method is to the few, it keeps the many safe and sound.

We are still progressing with the moat and we should soon have a five-foot wide trench around the walls. The Deceased, aka the Zombies, are learning, but slowly. Or perhaps through a sort of natural selection, the only ones to survive being those that are more aware and skilled. The Living have been picking them off for long enough for that development to make sense. But hopefully the wall-climbers will be deterred by a moat full of sharp implements and barbed wire, meaning we can spare some of the energy we were using to make arrows.

I'm not sure what happened to our latest radio signal. Perhaps the senders were driven off the map by an invasion they hadn't foreseen? Perhaps another tribe has taken over and hasn't yet, or never intends to, reconnect the signal. Whatever the cause, our last lifeline to the world and source of news has expired. It might be only a few days until another one emerges or one comes back online or it may be, as it was back in March, two months before we hear from anyone. We are familiar with this solitude by now and will continue to make progress. A couple of students have suggested sending a broadcast of our own, but the number of stations changing hands is suspicious to me. I believe there are some tribes that can track radio signals and will use it to invade and pillage forts like ours. And they may not be deterred by walls, arrows or even the moat. The Living may well have become more dangerous than the Deceased and I am not prepared to risk everything we have built.

I am not sure what tomorrow will hold.

Yours from the past,

Professor Travis Mole.

August 2nd, 2019.

Mole Camp, Texas (?).

"We are reporting movements from the Zombies. There are probably around... seventy of them... proper horde right there... they seem to be the smart ones too... Anyway, they're shuffling towards us, but I don't think they know there are people here yet. They are... very slow... very quiet. I don't know if they'll... make it over here or, you know, try and get in... I dunno if I've seen any so quiet for a while... we're definitely gonna be lucky to make it out without at least one... at least one trying to break in on us..."

Received August 2nd 2019 at around twelve noon. Copied verbatim from a radio transmission on frequency 107.5 FM, previously Camp F. Mercury.

"They are still moving. So many of them are now... bumping at the walls... no climbers yet... they seem to be unaware we are here... We... we have a climber... it's not fast... it's not fast... Sarge has shot it down with... an arrow, I think... yes, a wooden arrow... we don't have many weapons left, wood is good Sarge says... nobody else... nobody is on the walls but Sarge... the Zombie is down, but still scrambling... the rest are... retreating... I think... well, they're walking off... walking around us... they don't know we're here... it should be fine... many of them are probably out of earshot... once they are all gone we can get the others from the air shelter... We need to be quiet now... we'll... get back to you..."

Received August 2nd 2019 at around two twenty in the afternoon. Copied verbatim from a radio transmission on frequency 107.5 FM, previously Camp F. Mercury.

No further messages received by four pm on August 2nd 2019. So far I don't suspect the best or the worst. I need to know which way they were headed, but we may need to prepare for the horde so I have asked all lookouts to be vigilant tonight. The moat has been cancelled until further notice, so we can't have any more casualties. Smith has come to her senses and is working on the vehicles again, but Tyler may cause himself trouble. He is a skilled fighter, but as the other students learn more combat skills he becomes less useful. His arrogance and defiance could be the end of him if he does not adopt a lesser position in the tribe.

Yours from the past,

Professor Travis Mole.

"... they are gone... finally... they got in... four dead... one infected, evicted... we're... we're safe now... they headed South... if you're south of us, then please set up your guard... they're probably only two hours from the town and... we don't know where they'll go from then... we need to rebuild now... we will be back if we are not got first..."

Received August 2nd 2019 between sundown and midnight. Copied verbatim from a radio transmission on frequency 107.5 FM, previously Camp F. Mercury.

August 3rd, 2019.

Mole Camp, Texas (?).

We received no further messages, as expected, but we're already prepared. From our previous documents it looks like the former Camp F. Mercury was North from us. If this is from their camp radio and not just on the same frequency, we may sight some Deceased soon. We thought we were more than prepared, as we haven't had a raid in over two weeks and have been manufacturing weapons as fast as was realistically possible, but now we are working overtime. We have never seen a horde this big. Back in the cities there are probably this many, but they usually disperse as they leave the city. The hordes that have formed so far have been clusters of four or five, never this many. The only thing I can imagine that would cause this is if smaller hordes have gradually merged as they moved. We still don't know whether they communicate or how they follow each other. From the messages these ones seem to be not communicating at all, but we cannot be certain. It is best to be safe.

Smith has repaired two vehicles and Tyler has made himself useful making weapons. We can't send scouts out to uncover more tools or materials, so we have stripped some more furniture for arrows. We are also developing a colour code to help in retrieving the arrows. Green tailed ones have entered a Deceased human and are not to be retrieved, black tailed ones are in a human and can be reused. We can't be so wasteful anymore, not if this horde is an indication of things to come. Evans has hammered some more spear heads, but we need to get everyone focused on making wood arrows if we're to survive this. I will be talking to Thomas later to see if he can persuade Evans to work on arrows. Evans is a good kid, but his autism interferes with his ability to follow commands. Without Thomas he would have been a goner. It never ceases to astonish me how a marginally strong society both can afford to and deeply wants to protect its weak. This is what makes us human.

Yours from the past,
Professor Travis Mole.

August 4th, 2019.
Camp Mole, Texas (?).

This morning was uneventful, but all vehicles are now road-ready and we are better supplied with arrows now that everyone is making them. Even the guards are taking wood and whittle up with them to make their own arrows. Kelly and Luis have sighted the Undead a few times but we are not sure whether this is the horde we heard about. So far they have been dispersed and seem to be sightless, but there's a chance there are some fresher ones in the horde, who may still be sighted. They can definitely hear, as evidenced by their reaction to the gulls. Hopefully they will be distracted by the gulls and will not notice our fort.

But three Deceased don't mean there will be more. Hopefully it will turn out to be a coincidence.

Yours from the past,

Professor Travis Mole.

PS: Update, same day around 9 pm, just after sundown.

More sightings. The increase has begun to concern me. We are still worried there may be sighted ones on the way. It is quite likely that these are the start of the horde seen by Camp F. Mercury (or whatever their new name might be). If there are sighted ones then we need to keep the lights off, but this makes spotting them harder. Should we get any climbers we will need to turn the lights on to shoot them, but then? Half the camp is stationed on the walls as the other half sleeps. It is the only way we can be safe without using light. Even from my tower I can now see some movement near the wall, though the lighting is too weak to see how many. The weapons we have are plenty for those sighted so far, but how many is the darkness covering? The guard are still whittling arrows, but we all pray we will never have to use them. This could be what ends us, I hope these diaries and papers will last much further into the future than that. If you find these, you must spread and share them. It is my confident assertion that these papers, this knowledge, will be vital in the future.

Yours from the past,

Professor Travis Mole.

August 5th, 2019.

Camp Mole, Texas (?).

We made it through the night, but at sunrise when time came to change the guard we saw something that some of us haven't seen and the rest have not seen in months. There were far more than the original message implied. Probably close to a hundred in sight. Very spread out. We can't be certain that these are the same ones that were spotted by the others, but they are coming from the North and there are many of them. It is quite possible that hordes expand after they have formed a horde they will slowly drift away until there are just singles left again. Perhaps horde behaviour is a coincidence? If they are all tracking a scent or a sight or something, then perhaps they will accidentally end up walking together, in the same direction, without ever knowing where the others are, or at least not ever caring? I need to start mapping the routes followed by the Deceased and now is the best time. Perhaps we can see a trend in the routes they take and the routes they don't. If there is one, this could make travel and moving camp far safer than it currently is.

It is my belief that we will never rid ourselves of the plague that are the Deceased. There are simply too many of them and from what we have heard little to no research is underway. It is far more likely that we will learn to live among them. Just as AIDS or rubella once caused widespread panic and a change in human behaviours, so has this virus. Just as sightings of killer bees made us adapt, so have the Deceased. We must simply combine everything we know about medicine, war and pest control and eventually we will reach a time when the Deceased are not a problem for us and as few people suffer at their hands as are killed by bees or AIDS. We may be afraid of them because they resemble us, but so far none of them have shown enough intelligence to actually be considered human. They may be our bodies, but they are most likely being moved by parasitic organisms far less intelligent than we are. I firmly believe that we will be safe eventually and I hope that my tribe will make it that far.

As I was writing this Clara has made her way in here with excellent news. The Deceased are largely sticking to the road downwind from where our fort is. They have not seen us and look old enough that they may never see us. Even if the wind changes, they are unlikely to smell us either and will soon disappear down the road. The vast majority of them have already overlooked our little path and will hopefully continue to do so. We will need to remain vigilant overnight tonight also, but after that they will be long gone and we can return to life as normal. This is wonderful news and we have freshly repaired vehicles and a steady supply of arrows for our future outings.

Yours from the past,

Professor Travis Mole.

Professor Mole finished writing his diary and made his way steadily and wearily down from the tower. The vegetable patch was still doing well and the cabbages they had planted were attracting many small insects which could supply valuable protein and stop them from having to eat all their supplies of dried goat and coyote. Animals that were once considered pests were now vital food sources, as cabbages contained few calories and no protein, but would attract protein-rich insects. That was the one trouble with being so far out. There was no danger from other humans seeking their resources, but that was because the resources were scarce. Even their moat had to be waterless and full of shrapnel, as water was in very short supply. Professor Mole had on several occasions seen their water barrels drop almost low enough that they would have to move, but they generally found another spring, a well or experienced a blessed storm before the water dropped too low.

Nevertheless Professor Mole encouraged everyone to always be ready to leave. Raiders, hordes, famine and dehydration were all serious risks and they needed to be ready to pack the food and drive off. Most of their water and food was kept on their most pristine vehicle, a school bus that was not to be used unless there was an emergency. Smith regularly checked it to ensure it was ready to depart, sometimes looking at the engine five, six, seven times a day. Thinking of Smith brought Tyler's comments back to mind. In a way, he admired Tyler's knowledge and forwardness. But he also found the boy to lack commutative, logical thought. Of course the tribe would need to breed to survive. But in their present situation a pregnant woman or a child would be nothing but a burden. Besides that, Smith was a fine mechanic, not the best but very good and the only one they had. Should she be lost to pregnancy or childbirth they would essentially be stranded. This was why Professor Mole had been opposed to the elimination of pornography by the tribe. The vote had been swayed by a number of more moral men along with the women, and the leader at the time had upheld their vote, but Mole had always known it would bring trouble. Young, virile men like Tyler needed an outlet, a release, and although they did not need it, without visual stimulation some would turn to fantasies about the young, healthy, pretty women they had in the tribe. It was only natural. But from these desires a sort of mind fog was born and being one of the most obviously high-testosterone men in the tribe, if not the one with the highest testosterone, Tyler was suffering the most. He was still rational enough that rape, even if it had crossed his mind, was still deemed unsafe and Professor Mole doubted that anyone there would turn to such drastic measures, at least not against their fellow tribeswomen. But he was starting to rationalize his desire into something practical and that was a thought pattern that could become dangerous. Children were not desirable at this stage and should Tyler make another such remark or attempt to persuade any of the women he would need to be reprimanded and given something more practical to use his energy on, lest the tribe turn on him. Or, worse, lest they give into him...

Professor Mole finished climbing the ladder up the wall and looked around himself. It was desolate, except for the slowly ambling horde in the distance, like a mass of insects, and a number of the Deceased still making their way past them, following down the road. Everyone knew better than to speak, move suddenly or make any other obvious noise at this time, so Thomas simply rested his hand on the Professor's shoulder as a sign of camaraderie. At first nobody had been willing to engage in physical contact, but Professor Mole had convinced them of the merits to bonding. He was confident that their tribe was as close as it was from the physical contact they engaged in, especially the additional contact the men made with each other. A simple hand on a back or shoulder made all the difference and in-group fighting was restricted to women's hormonal shifts and men displaying excessive arrogance or dominance.

Having checked the situation and made further note of the paths most of the Deceased were following, Professor Mole slowly made his way back down and into the small library and copy room that had been made. Clara, his personal secretary of sorts, had stopped whittling arrows and was busily making a fifth copy of his diary. Without interrupting her, he picked up the pages she had already noted, nodded and made his way outside with them. He made his way to where the whittlers were resting and sat among them. This was one of the few areas with low sound carrying, which meant it was perfect for noisy work, like cutting the rough form of the arrows, metal work and, of course, reading. The whittlers welcomed him and fell silent, ready to hear him read from the first book for what seemed like the hundredth time. They had long grown used to this and enjoyed it. It was the only story, besides short fairytales and enactments of films memorized long ago, that they could still share. And it held a special importance as the story of them.

January 25th, 2019.
St Augustine's Campus, Yale University.
I am beginning this diary for one reason and one reason only. I believe we are on the dawn of a new era, of a great historical event and a shift the likes of which the world has not seen in a very, very long time.

Just as the Black Death in Europe and the bomb on Hiroshima, these events will one day be viewed as the catalyst for a radically different nation, possibly a radically different world, although it may be contained by then.

The facts, as far as we have been told, are as follow:

1: A disease has broken out across the South East of the United States. This disease is spreading quickly.

2: The effects of this disease are similar to those of some parasitic organisms. These organisms affect the host's brain and direct it until its body dies and the parasite dies with it. These organisms are usually fungal and direct the host to the best place from which to emit spores, ensuring the survival of its genetics.

3: This disease is the first of its kind observed in any higher mammal, let alone humans, and the nature of the parasite (if, indeed, there is one) is unknown.

4: The original source of the disease appears to be a family by the name of Ferry, however how they contracted it is unknown, as they could not be reasoned with or saved and had to be terminated before they could tell anyone.

5: The current status is that some towns and villages are being evacuated, however everywhere else is encouraged to continue as normal. Some families have already fled the country and some nations are refusing US migrants.

I believe that these sightings and infections will only increase in number and the intervals will become shorter. There is no way of containing this until it is known what exactly this is. Until then, it's safe to assume that most of the continent will fall to it.

As it stands, many nearby towns and cities have already been evacuated. I believe ours will be next, based on the trends. It seems that evacuation is systematic, not total, to contain the panic and not clog the roads. It is very likely that we will be evacuated tomorrow and I do not know what the future holds for us then. Life is uncertain indeed.

I hope my students will make it, but as citizens are currently being evacuated by neighbourhood it is unlikely that I will see them for a very long time.

I am beginning this diary to document what I believe will be inevitable and to document it from the start. I hope I will see the day when all this passes, but if I do not, I at least hope my diary will assist future historians in piecing together what may become a very dark and undocumented time.

Yours from the past,
Professor Travis Mole.

January 26th, 2019.
Evacuation caravan 456, vehicle D.

As predicted, we were evacuated today. I guess studying population demographics has its uses. I had packed well in advance, unlike many of my neighbours who scrambled to collect their belongings and were dismayed to find what they could not bring. Fortunately I had also checked the evacuation lists and have brought everything useful with me. High calorie tinned foods, dried foods, matches, firelighters, my notebooks and pencils, a radio, a sewing box, a few kitchen tools and some antibiotics and throat medicines. Not much, or as much as I would have collected if I had worked it out sooner, but it will serve me well. The Sargent, a Sargent Pines or something of the likes, seems to have taken a liking to me on account of my preparedness and is happy to share his ration packs and fresh fares with me, to spare my durable foods. He has already informed me in private, or the relative privacy of a bathroom break, that nobody has any idea what's happening, not even his commanding officers. They are just rounding us up and walking us out and nobody knows why, where or for what.

It's possible that we're being taken somewhere safe. Or that we're too close to the disease areas and will be terminated. But it's also possible that we're being distracted by all these evacuations, that they're a diversion to stop us from noticing something. But all this is mere speculation. I don't know and have no reason to believe any theory over any other. My mind is running wild in the absence of solid information, evidence, anything.

If we are being taken to an evacuation camp I hope they have some use for an old historian like myself. As an aside, at forty nine I never thought of myself as old until today. Funny how disaster does that. One day I'm middle aged, very fit and might have another forty nine ahead of me if I'm lucky. The next day I'm at risk of competing against these twenty year olds and I feel like an antique. I would not be able to keep up with them if this goes the way history says it will. I hope I am either out of the country or making myself very useful by then, because not many people will have much use for an old man.

But I am getting ahead. We will probably be fine. Evacuations are rarely traps or tricks. It may be a distraction, but it is still moving us away from the outbreak and between us we still have a lot of food and weapons. We are very safe for now. It won't be long before we stop for the night, if we do stop, as the sun is setting. Perhaps we will keep driving through the night, if that is a wise option. I know far too little about current military and emergency strategies to make an educated remark on it. What I do know is that soon it will be too dark to write and I will have to end today at that.

Yours from the past,
Professor Travis Mole.

January 30th, 2019.
Sargent Pinez's refugee group, Army Base. Texas border (maybe).

Things have not gone well and the pace has been too quick for me to keep writing this diary. As we sit around our camp fire, I will fill this in as best I can from memory, but may future readers take note that none of this is fresh and the order and significance may be affected by my memory and shock.

The night of the 26th was as uneventful as we had expected, as was the morning of the 27th. But at midday on the 27th we stopped for a bathroom break and were attacked by some sort of a rebel convoy. A number of off road vehicles, including some dirt bikes and a van, pulled up around us. It was pretty obvious they were locking us in, but the military stood their ground. The decision would have been correct in any other situation, but it turns out these rebels had RPGs and grenades. The vehicles were largely destroyed. We watched from the toilet area but anyone who moved in to rescue the burning victims was shot.. I do not wish to recall any further.

The rebels' tactics were highly ineffective. In destroying our caravan they had also destroyed most of the food, half the vehicles and our fuel and water supplies. Then they chose to take the survivors captive, a decision I am very thankful of. Had they left us out in the desert we would have died, but we were fortunate enough to become their slaves of sorts. I don't know whether they thought they could sell us, make us work or eat us, but their flawed reasoning saved eight lives that day.

Their final error was in their choice of food. The fires destroyed food packets, melted water bottles, evaporated other liquids and exploded cans. Almost everything we could eat was ruined. So they turned to the corpses. It felt unthinkable to us at the time, but we did not know how long they had gone without food. For us, a few hours of hunger were not enough to drive us to such measures and my own concerns kept me from eating undercooked human flesh. At first nothing seemed amiss, but that night we awoke to the sound of gunfire. It appears that either some of the rebels were already infected or that one of the bodies was infected. The first is more likely than the latter, as I'm not sure how well the disease survives charring. But some of the flesh was raw and the incubation period didn't seem right, so the latter is also very likely. Either way, they were already turning and their comrades were shooting them. Between the Deceased, the gunfire and the chaos, Sargent Pinez managed to isolate a vehicle, load all the captives into it and drive away. He had already identified the vehicle with the most fuel and water at the start and was ready to move as soon as he saw an opportunity. He drove us a great distance in a zig zag, eventually settling us on another road before setting up camp for the night.

On the 28th we rose early, with the run, and started moving. Many bags were discovered to have been stolen and kept on this vehicle before the attacks so we found some tins of food and my bag with all my supplies. Sargent Pinez seemed intent on making me appear valuable. He understands my concerns regarding my age, as I am the most senior of the group by around a decade and a half. I need to look useful to these young people or I may not make it. Some had already mentioned dead weight and I feared that I was being seen that way, despite my fitness and survival knowledge.

We travelled very far over that one day, much faster than we had in the caravan, and Sargent explained that he was on his way to a base. It was not our original destination, but it would be much safer than the desert or the convoy's actual route, which he wasn't that familiar with.

We set up camp again that night and resumed driving on the 29th. The drive remained uneventful, the day was not quite long enough and I offered to drive the night shift, which allowed us to finally reach the base. They welcomed us and fed us and we explained everything we knew before going to sleep.

I am writing this on the morning of January 30th, over what feels like my first cup of coffee in centuries and what may be my last. Coffee is scarce and only offered to newcomers, night shift and shocked people. We seem to be safe so far, all eight of us.

Besides myself and Sargent, there is Anna, a pregnant woman, and her son Joseph, who looks around five. If we can stay here they may do well. They are both very lucky to be alive, as Anna had wanted Joseph to go to the toilet just outside the van. Joseph was shy and they left a little further, missing the explosions. There is a middle aged couple, Clara and Michael, and a recent widow by the name of Smith. All of them had left to smoke and all had lost family in the blasts. Clara and Michael had lost their two sons and their daughter, having left them at the caravan under the impression it was safer. Smith, from what we had gathered, had left her infant son with her husband as she went to smoke, to not expose the child to the fumes, I assume. The only one left is Tyler, a young man, possibly just a teenager, who does not speak much. Hopefully we can all stay here and we will be safe, but I know we can't stay here forever.

Yours from the past,
Professor Travis Mole.

January 31st, 2019.
Sargent Pinez's refugee group, Army Base. Texas border (maybe).

It seems to be genuinely safe here. There is plenty of food to go around, we are all being made to earn our keep but this also means we are now armed and trained in how to use our weapons. Only Anna refuses to use a weapon to kill, but she is unlikely to be used in her current state and has therefore not been persuaded. I don't think this is a wise move, but in the present environment I'm not sure what would be considered a good move for a visibly pregnant woman.

So far it looks like we're fixed here. There are plenty of supplies to go around, the area is enforced, the Base was not marked. Our chances of another rebel raid are highly unlikely and even in that event, we're more than armed to defeat them and the buildings are far stronger than the caravan vehicles were.

Now that we're secure emotions and tension are running high as everyone comes to terms with what has happened. I know I lost everyone I knew from my neighbourhood, but it hasn't hit me yet. Perhaps at my age you start getting ready to see people die, or perhaps I am just hardened by my knowledge that this is all now inevitable, but I haven't felt the loss yet.

We have been told that we will be working on packing some bunkers and some vehicles in case an emergency strikes that requires either. This is a smart solution to the risk of attack. I am happy to put my trust entirely in these people's hands. I may as well be, as I do not have any other option.

Everyone else is less happy with the decision. It's a strange mix between the lust for independence our country has prized for so long and a sort of primitive, tribal democracy that can't end well. We don't need dissent at this point, but everyone has their complaint. Anna won't kill anyone and is defiant of the army's authority, Clara and Michael are eager to move on and keep running, Smith seems to either be in deepest grief of completely absorbed in her own thoughts and Tyler has become outspoken and is trying to take control of the situation. This feels like a recipe for disaster and I am not sure it will resolve itself through democracy or through force.

Yours from the past,

Professor Travis Mole.

February 16th, 2019.

Sargent Pinez's refugee group, Camp College Campus. Texas (maybe).

I have lost many pages in the chaos, but this is what little I can recall of the past two weeks.

As I suspected, the conflict was too much. Michael packed his bags and left shortly after my last entry. He heard a radio report about the advance of the Deceased, panicked, and made his way out into the desert without thinking twice. Clara refused to join him, despite his attempts at coercing and threatening her. She was distraught that he had left her and could not be consoled for many days.

A couple of days later, following further reports, Sargent Pinez decided it was time to move camp. There were a total of twenty seven of us in the convoy, but we moved much faster than the caravan. We located a university campus of sorts, a very old building, just outside a small town that was almost entirely deserted. I never thought I would be back at a university again! There were some others already holed in there and we set up to spend the night. Sargent Pinez managed to quickly bring order to everyone and it seems to be running much more smoothly than it had at the Base.

We are currently busy building up the place and trying to establish a radio connection, although it now seems impossible. There is no signal for miles and we are very isolated. Sargent Pinez says this is both good and bad, as we are very safe, but also very lonely. It looked like he felt his statement was wise, but how wise I am not sure. Everyone seems to adore him, though, so he is doing something right.

Yours from the past,
Professor Travis Mole.

February 17th, 2019.
Camp College Campus, formerly Sargent Pinez's refugee group, Texas (?).

Yesterday's events shook us all, but we are still striving to build the community Sargent Pinez thought we needed. He was a wise man and will be remembered by all.

Yesterday around five or six in the afternoon, food poisoning caused Anna to enter early labour. She refused to be moved from the gate where she lay and was in obvious pain. At first we tried to help her, but then, as though from nowhere, the Deceased emerged. They seemed drawn by her cries, or by the smell of her broken waters and her blood, or possibly both. We picked her up and carried her inside, reinforcing the barrier. The stress from the movement may have caused her to lose her baby, as it was stillborn.

Our efforts to enforce the gates were as futile as our efforts to revive the child. As Anna wept and cried and mourned, the Deceased were drawn like flies until eventually the pressure of them all on the gate caused it to fall in. Sargent Pinez rallied everyone together and got those with arms to hold off the Deceased as the unarmed were herded into some more robust rooms and instructed to remain quiet. We're not sure what happened between carrying the vulnerable into these rooms and when the doors burst open, but as the last two men entered the room and locked the door, we caught a glimpse of the Deceased attacking Pinez and the other three men. We stayed holed up until this morning. When we emerged there was only one Deceased left, so we killed and removed it swiftly. We can only assume Pinez and the others were infected and wandered off with the rest of the horde. We hope neither of the surviving men turn out to be infected too.

Yours from the past,

Professor Travis Mole.

February 18th, 2019.

Camp College Campus, Texas (?).

The new order has not yet been established and I don't think it will be for a while. Humans are naturally somewhat democratic and none of us are yet prepared to replace Sargent Pinez. However, by some stroke of luck, Pinez's radio system is picking up on some transmissions. We have so far found two radio stations, a walkie talkie range and another ham radio.

We have not yet reached any agreement on what to do about the walkie talkie or the other radio. Some say that we need to make contact, that the more the better and we should save those who are as desperate as ourselves. However many of us, especially those who had experienced raids, violence and theft, were more wary of inviting strangers or of disclosing our location via radio.

Until we are comfortable to make any decisions on making contact, we are comforting ourselves with the news. Not that there is much comfort to it. The disease is spreading, nobody knows how to cure or contain it and there is very little information about how it spreads except that it seems to be borne in the blood. We must make great effort to not touch the blood of the deceased from now on...

Professor Mole's reading could not go on after this point. The alarm had been sounded. Or, rather, Clara had burst in through the door calling them to the walls.

Everyone ran to get their crossbows and green arrows and made their way to the walls, where the others were firing arrows into the horde that had apparently came from nowhere and begun trying to scale the wall. None of these were fresh, but they seemed to be seeing the world around them, or perceiving it, just as well without eyes as their adversaries could perceive it with eyes. Everyone aimed for the heads and the chests, hoping to rupture the brain or lungs and bring the creatures to a halt. They didn't know why these attacks worked and pain did not, but they now relied on this knowledge.

This horde was genuinely something they hadn't seen before and Professor Mole felt uneasy seeing them scale. Then he realized why. This was the horde from before. They had turned around and attacked the camp just as they let their guard down. A novice's error and a fatal one if they were less prepared. This is probably what had caught the new Camp F. Mercury inhabitants by surprise. These Deceased, unlike the others before them, were using strategies. They had worked out a way around their lack of eyesight and slight loss of smell and had worked out a way of deceiving the Living humans that had built forts. There was no doubt about it now, they weren't just deselecting the inefficient ones. This was entirely new behaviour, not yet documented and never seen by Professor Mole and his camp.

Despite the new developments in the Deceased, Professor Mole's students managed to drive them back and kill most if not all of them. The remaining few, as the majority were massacred, seemed to lose the binding of the spell they were under and gradually regressed to their more primitive behaviours.

It was as though they had a hive mind. The hordes may be forming casually or purposefully and they may be drifting apart, but the more of them there were together, the more advanced their strategies became.

And what was the end goal? The only one Professor Mole could imagine was that of spreading the disease's genetic materials. Spreading the disease into more hosts. That meant the Deceased were actively seeking out the Living and were learning to better track and defeat their prey. To keep ahead of them, Professor Mole would have to train his students further. And he wasn't sure whether he was ready for that. To adapt they had to learn from history, but they also had to learn in the present. He summoned everyone together that afternoon.

"Students, I'm here to tell you, in no uncertain terms, that we need a new leader. Not to take over from me, as my expertise and wisdom is still, in my unhumble opinion, invaluable." He paused as a few people laughed, defusing the tension that had somehow built in the room. "However, I think the latest horde attack has shown us a lot. It has shown us how strong we have become, but also that we need to keep developing. Like lions and zebras on the plains and like the Goths and the Romans, we are playing a game of catchup with the Deceased. They make progress and we make progress and they make progress again. And it seems that they are starting to progress once more. My methods are good provided that the Deceased remain mindless animals, but what if they were able to access more of their human intelligence, what then?"

The following silence gave him a chance to see the whole room turn pale. But that was important. He remained quiet.

"Then we need soldiers, don't we?" Tyler replied with his usual confidence almost restored except for a slight shake to his voice.

"Yes, that is what we need. And I'm a teacher, at the end of the day. I can teach you about the military strategies of great past soldiers, but I can't teach you actual warfare tactics, which is where our new leader comes in. As the most skilled and responsible, in my unhumble observations, of the surviving soldiers, I would like to see Thomas work by my side in helping us fight off the Deceased. We need to remain safe and Thomas is one of the few men, or women, I can trust to stay strong in this position. What say you, Thomas?"

"I accept." Thomas said unhesitatingly. He clearly knew the role had its risks, but he had always said that he didn't join the army because he was afraid of risks. Professor Mole was just making him put his money where his mouth was.

"And what say you, students?" The room cheered and Professor Mole smiled. "Thank you, it's decided. Now, I think it's time for some of us to get some sleep." With that, he left the room, making a mental note to add this to his diary for posterity before he went to bed. Everything was for posterity.

Everything would become history someday.